## "I'm not positive, but I think we're being followed."

"It's a dark sedan, either black or navy blue," Claire confirmed. "There are at least two people in it. How long have they been following us?"

"I spotted them a few blocks from the park," Alex said. "But there were a lot of people there. A lot of people coming and going. It wasn't until this last turnoff that I knew for sure."

"They couldn't go after us in the park. There were too many people. And—"

"And it wouldn't fit into the scenario Xavier has built around you being the murderer if someone took you out in such a public place. It would look too suspicious."

Claire winced. If Xavier got to her, if he killed her, he would make sure there were no witnesses.

"We're certainly not in a public place now." Claire eyed the empty road ahead with trepidation.

"Here they come," Alex said under his breath. He reached for his Glock. "Hold on tight," he said to Claire. "We're going for a ride."

**Amity Steffen** lives in northern Minnesota with her two boys and two spoiled cats. She's a voracious reader and a novice baker. She enjoys watching her sons play baseball in the summer and would rather stay indoors in the winter. She's worked in the education field for more years than she cares to count, but writing has always been her passion. Amity loves connecting with readers, so please visit her at Facebook.com/amitysteffenauthor.

### Books by Amity Steffen

### Love Inspired Suspense

*Reunion on the Run*

# REUNION ON THE RUN

## AMITY STEFFEN

**❖ HARLEQUIN®** LOVE INSPIRED® SUSPENSE

Recycling programs
for this product may
not exist in your area.

LOVE INSPIRED BOOKS

ISBN-13: 978-1-335-23206-9

Reunion on the Run

www.Harlequin.com

Printed in U.S.A.

Judge not, and ye shall not be judged:
condemn not, and ye shall not be condemned:
forgive and ye shall be forgiven.
—*Luke* 6:37

For my boys, Zack and Nick. I'm so proud of you and I'm so blessed to be your mom. I know your dad is watching over you, every bit as proud of you as I am.

# ONE

Roscoe's fierce growl sent a chill skittering down Claire Mitchell's spine. She slid back from the rickety table, bouncing to her feet as her dog continued to give his warning. It was gloomy in the old one-room hunting shack. A kerosene lantern cast a hazy glow over the notes she studied. She'd been on the run for weeks. From the outside, the shack should look unoccupied. The nights had become chilly but she hadn't indulged in the luxury of a fire, too worried the smoke would give her away. There were only four windows in the small dwelling, one on each wall. She'd had to make do with what she'd been able to scrounge up. Threadbare bath towels had been tacked over each pane. They should block the minimal kerosene light, even in the evenings.

It wasn't dark yet but would be soon. Her heart slammed against her rib cage, each thump pushing ice through her veins. She'd been telling herself if someone found her, she was prepared. She'd almost believed the lie.

She was a murder suspect.

But she was *not* a worthy adversary of Xavier Ambrose's hired henchmen.

Roscoe growled again. Mild-mannered and loving most of the time, rottweilers were fiercely loyal protectors. Having his companionship and protection eased her mind, making it worth the extra trouble to keep him with her.

His sturdy body guarded the door, the only way in—or out—of the shack. His teeth were bared and his posture rigid. There was no need for her to try to peek outside to confirm that she was about to be ambushed. Roscoe's change in demeanor made it clear.

*"Hush!"* She hissed the word under her breath. She was grateful the dog was well-trained, courtesy of Alex Vasquez, her ex-fiancé. He wouldn't bark, giving away the fact that she wasn't alone in the shack. She couldn't chance the intruders hearing him growl, either. Roscoe was her best chance at escape.

With trembling hands Claire shoved the notes she'd been working on into the backpack that rested at the center of the table. It cost her precious seconds, but the contents were even more precious. She slipped the backpack over her shoulders. She tugged at the cord around her neck, finding her poor excuse for a weapon at the end of it. Palming the vial of pepper spray, she snuffed out the flame in the lantern.

Roscoe huffed, his huge body nimbly pacing back and forth in front of the doorway.

Claire darted over to him. She pressed herself against the rough plank wall of the shack. Not for the first time she futilely wished the place had another escape route. The windows were small and simple, nothing more than single panes of glass built into the frames. They would need to be shattered because they couldn't be wedged open. She wouldn't risk the noise announcing an escape attempt, nor would she risk being sliced to ribbons trying to squeeze through the small space.

"Heel." The command was barely a whisper. Roscoe gave her a bewildered look before he complied.

The doorknob jiggled. It sounded like a cannon against the silence.

She had been under no illusion that she would be safe here indefinitely. That hadn't stopped her from hoping for more time. With limited resources, two weeks hadn't been nearly long enough to compile the evidence she needed to clear her name.

"Claire, we know you're in there," a deep, gravelly voice taunted from the other side. "Open up and we'll take it easy on you."

A second menacing voice warned, "Make us come in after you, and you might not live to regret it."

It was an empty threat. She was well aware of the fact that she might not live to regret it either way.

Terror mingled with the intense determination to stay alive. A hard edge dug into her palm as she held her hand at eye level, poised and steady.

Mia's precious face flashed through her mind. Her dark curls, her spunky smile. It had been far too long since she'd been able to give her three-year-old daughter a hug. A kiss. Far too many nights had passed without reading her a bedtime story.

For Mia, she had to get out of this mess. She would not leave her daughter parentless.

The thin wood shuddered as a body slammed into it.

Roscoe whined as he crouched, ready to attack.

*Please Lord, please Lord, please Lord*, Claire silently prayed. She could string together nothing more coherent than this simple, frantic prayer. She trusted He knew what she was asking, even if she was far too panicked to find the right words to say.

Another assault shook the entire shack. The flimsy door splintered at the bottom.

Claire gritted her teeth and braced for the inevitable. She pressed herself as tightly as she could against the wall.

When it shattered, pieces of wood flying everywhere, she was ready.

Her first attacker blinked in surprise, his eyes trying to adjust to the gloom. He clearly did not expect Claire to be ready to face him head-on. She squeezed the trigger before he could swing his gun her way. He screamed in agony as the pepper spray shot out of the canister she held. A gun clattered at her feet. She kicked it, sending it flying across the cabin to land under the battered couch.

Roscoe, snuffling and sneezing from the mist in the air, leaped at the second man before he could enter the cramped space. He slammed him to the ground as his gun went off. The window next to the door shattered, spraying glass that narrowly missed Claire.

The first man clawed at his face, cursing and writhing in pain. The second man cried out, his gun falling to his side as Roscoe latched onto his forearm. The dog stood over him, teeth clenched tightly as the man tried to push him off.

Claire stepped out of the cabin and gasped, sucking in fresh air. Though she'd used the stickier, gel-type pepper spray, the fumes still lingered. She blinked hard a few times, clearing her vision but not allowing herself a moment to slow down.

"Heel!" Claire commanded after she grabbed the second gun and tossed it into the trees. Roscoe let go of his target and bounced to her side. Claire was ready. The moment Roscoe was out of her way, she shot off what was left of the pepper spray. The second man shrieked, his cries melding with his cohort's.

A third figure, dressed in black, emerged from the tree line. He shouted something at her, probably her name, but it was mostly drowned out by the sound of her heartbeat crashing through her ears.

"Come." She grated out the stern command, unwilling to let Roscoe go after the newest threat. These thugs worked for the man who'd had Jared, her husband, murdered. She knew they wouldn't hesitate to shoot a dog.

Claire took off at a dead run, circling to the backside of the cabin. She lacked brute strength and she was outnumbered. If she'd known there was a third henchman, one who was able to pursue her, she may have been tempted to keep the gun. It was too late now. She prayed she hadn't made a grave mistake. She had God on her side. He had brought her this far, she was counting on Him to bring her the rest of the way.

Her hiking boots pounded across the thin edge of lawn before she charged full-speed into the thick copse of trees. The sun had just slipped past the horizon, plunging the world into the murky gray of twilight. Darkness would work to her advantage. She knew these woods. She'd already planned her escape through them.

Adrenaline spilled through her body, making it easy to push ahead. Her heart pounded chaotically and her spine tingled, anticipating a bullet at any moment. She knew the two men at her door would be down and out for several minutes. The third man posed an enormous threat.

She tore through the dense forest, dodging trees, leaping over fallen logs. Pine boughs and oak branches slapped at her, tore at her skin. Roscoe obediently raced alongside her.

*When you go through deep waters, I will be with you.*

This had become her mantra. She was in about as deep as she could get. She was drowning in troubles but it gave her comfort to know she was never alone. He was always by her side.

She didn't dare a glance over her shoulder. She couldn't waste precious seconds by slowing down, and if she looked while running she'd likely crash into a tree. It didn't matter. She didn't need to look. Claire had no doubt she was being pursued. She didn't have to see him to know. She could *feel* his presence behind her. This knowledge drove her to move even faster.

Her escape plan was on a constant loop, playing through her mind. Up ahead the woods were bisected by an overgrown logging trail. If she continued to run straight, she'd hit the trail eventually. The trail led to the gravel road that would ultimately spill onto a county road leading to the highway.

Freedom was within her reach.

If only she didn't trip, crash into a tree or get shot in the back first.

"Claire!" The harshness of her name grated out in frustration caused a sharp whimper of surprise to bubble up in her throat. She hadn't realized her pursuer was so close. Her skin broke out in a chilled sweat and it had nothing to do with exertion. Her legs burned, and her lungs ached. She couldn't move any faster. Even if she made it to the logging trail, with her pursuer so close, she'd never have the extra minutes she desperately needed to get away.

Now that she was aware of his nearness, she could hear branches snapping and footsteps racing up behind her.

She winced, fully prepared to be taken down.

The man's voice rang out again. Louder, clearer. Closer this time. *"Roscoe! Come!"*

The sharp command was like a mental punch to the gut. She whirled reflexively, nearly tripping over her own feet at the sound of the unexpected voice. It was doubtful Xavier's men knew the name of her dog. Even more doubtful they'd take the time to toss out a command. Not when they had an arsenal at their disposal. And that voice... It caused her heart to rattle because it was so familiar. Yet impossible.

The dog yipped as his agile body changed course. He circled around, leaping up, plastering his feet against the chest of their pursuer. The man was prepared. He braced himself so the enormous dog didn't take him down. One hand gripped the dog. The other hand gripped a firearm.

Roscoe's massive form blocked Claire's view of his face. But she'd caught a glimpse. Just a glimpse of that bronzed skin, the charcoal hair and those coffee-colored eyes.

Her mind had to be playing tricks on her. Maybe the stress she was under was messing with her mental state. Had she finally cracked under the pressure? Was she hallucinating? She felt she had to be.

Now that she'd skidded to a stop, her legs felt like rubber. She willed them to move. Taking a step backward, she didn't take her eyes off the dog and man. Only a few seconds passed but it felt like an eternity before the man gently pushed the dog aside.

Roscoe landed on all fours with a disappointed whine.

She had been prepared, as prepared as she could have been, for Xavier's men.

But as the weeks dragged by, she hadn't prepared for herself for this. Hadn't been prepared for *him*. His presence stole what little was left of her breath, leaving her gasping. Her already wobbly legs threatened to give out and send her toppling.

She might as well have been looking at a mirage because Alex Vasquez was the absolute last man she'd expected to see.

"Alex?" Claire gasped for breath as she pressed a hand against her chest. Her gaze slid over his shoulder, scanning the woods behind him. "What are you doing here? How…? Why…?"

"Your sister sent me."

Her eyes widened at the mention of Beth.

"I don't have time to explain." He cast a glance over his shoulder, as well. He'd seen Claire take down two men. He couldn't have been more impressed. But he knew they wouldn't be down indefinitely. He would've liked to have incapacitated them, tied them up, let the law deal with them, but in doing so he would've lost Claire. He'd had to make a split-second judgment call. Chasing after her had definitely been the right choice. If he'd lost her, he was certain he wouldn't have found her again. "We need to get out of here."

Claire pivoted and took off again. He jogged after her.

"I have a vehicle parked back there," he explained. "We need to loop around the cabin, keep a wide berth and head to the west."

"And risk running into Xavier's men again? No." Her tone was firm.

"What do you suggest we do?" He wasn't really expecting an answer, but he was on board with putting more distance between them and the men. It would be dark soon. Nighttime would offer them the cover they needed to skirt back around, as he'd suggested.

He easily kept pace with her, though she was moving at a steady clip.

She shot him a look that was full of questions. He was

relieved she didn't press him for answers. He'd give them to her eventually, but at the moment they had more urgent matters to deal with.

They had to get out of these woods.

"I'm not going back that way. We don't know that those men were alone. More could be coming."

He'd thought of the possibility, as well, but hadn't wanted to mention it.

She slowed as the woods thinned. Seconds later they emerged from the trees. Claire cut a sharp left and he followed. Their feet pounded in unison against the hard-packed trail. He scanned the area, always on the lookout.

Up ahead he spotted a gray tarp draped over a hulking object. It looked out of place this deep in the woods.

"Is that part of your getaway plan?"

"Yes."

Alex had no doubt the tarp covered a vehicle. He reached it first and tugged the covering to the side. A rusted-out Jeep Wrangler appeared. At one time it must've been a vibrant shade of red. Now what was left of the faded paint was barely visible. The thing had to be at least a quarter of a century old. It had a canvas top rather than a hard top. The sort that could be removed, convertible style. The canvas was tattered but in good enough shape to offer protection from the elements.

"I hope this thing runs," he mumbled.

"Of course it runs." She tugged a key chain holding a single key out of her pocket.

Claire, he realized, was incredibly resourceful. Accused of killing her husband of nearly a year—the man she'd married after Alex had broken off their engagement over three years ago—she'd managed to evade law enforcement for weeks. Maybe that wasn't an attribute he should be proud of, but he was.

He knew now was not the time to be struck by her beauty, yet he couldn't help himself. He hadn't seen her for years. She hadn't aged, not that he could tell. If anything, she looked younger. Her face looked gaunt, probably from the stress she'd been under. Her cheeks were rosy. Her long auburn hair had been chopped into a shaggy cut and dyed black. Fire flashed in her green eyes when she caught him staring.

She nudged him to the side as she reached for the driver's door. He blocked her way and held out a hand.

"Give me the key."

"No." She tried to reach around him.

"Hand it over, Claire. We don't have time to argue. If we get pulled over, do you really want a cop to see your name on the license?"

"Do you plan on getting pulled over?"

"Did you plan on being framed for your husband's murder?"

The words seemed to echo as they hung in the air. He wanted to take them back. He hadn't meant to sound so callous. Before he could apologize, Claire clenched her jaw and slammed the key into his palm.

He opened the door, allowing Roscoe to leap into the back seat. He slid into the driver's seat as Claire flung open the opposite door and scrambled in.

Alex jammed the key into the ignition. True to Claire's word, the old beast roared to life. With one final visual sweep of the woods, he put the vehicle in gear and sped down the rutted trail. If the men had followed, there was a chance they'd gotten themselves lost in the thick woods. The Jeep's engine would alert them to what direction their quarry had headed. He left the headlights off, not wanting to make it any easier for them.

Claire braced her hands against the dash as the Jeep bounced over the rough terrain.

"The gravel road intersects around the next corner. Take a left," she instructed. "Taking a right will bring us back to the hunting shack. If we head the other way, it'll lead us to the interstate."

The Jeep slid to a stop as they emerged from the tree line. Alex did a quick scan for oncoming traffic before tearing onto the deserted road. The Jeep fishtailed on the gravel, but he easily kept control.

A vehicle turned onto the road ahead of them. Its headlights sliced into the night. The Jeep's headlights were still off. Alex knew he was taking a risk. It was one he was willing to take.

"I have a bad feeling about this." Claire's tone was tense. "There's almost never traffic on this road."

The vehicle barreled toward them. With its headlights shining, it was impossible to determine the make.

In the past, Alex had wronged Claire in more ways than he could count. He wasn't about to add another mistake to that list.

"Hold on tight."

"I am," she said through clenched teeth.

His spine stiffened as he gripped the steering wheel. Claire wasn't the only one who had a bad feeling. When the oversize SUV swung into their lane, skidding sideways, blocking both lanes of traffic on the narrow road, Alex was ready.

He had only an instant to decide if he was going to crash into it, cut in front of it or loop around the back. He hit the gas. The Jeep sped forward as he cut behind it. The driver likely expected Alex to stay in his own lane, cutting down to the ditch in front. If he did that, the driver would only have to hit the gas to take them out.

Alex did the opposite. He cut into the other lane, tore down into the ditch and passed on the backside. By the time the driver wrenched into Reverse, they had cut back onto the road.

Claire's head whipped around to look out the back window. "He's trying to turn around."

Alex glanced in the rearview mirror. The SUV had angled into the oncoming lane as it tried to cut the Jeep off. The driver backed into the ditch but had to pull ahead again. He'd be tied up with the back-and-forth motion as he tried to turn around.

Taking advantage of the other driver's incompetence, Alex sped toward the interstate. He wasn't sure it was the best plan of action. This time of night, traffic would be pretty light. As they reached a crossroads he wrenched the steering wheel to the right. This stretch of road was lined with thick pines.

It was dark now, but in the glow of the moonlight he could make out mailboxes intermittently dotted along the road. He glanced in the rearview mirror.

"They haven't turned yet," Claire said. "They will any minute, though. They'd just turned around when you turned off."

"Perfect," Alex said under his breath.

They passed another crossroads. Alex split his gaze between the road in front and the road behind. He knew Claire was right. Any second now the other vehicle would be barreling after them. They had an impressive lead, but he'd rather lose the men for good sooner rather than later.

He made a decision he hoped he wouldn't regret. He wrenched the steering wheel and whipped into a long, winding driveway. Alex thought he glimpsed headlights slicing around the corner that was now a good distance back. He coasted down the driveway, grateful the house wasn't visible from the road.

"What are you doing?" Claire's panicked tone was laced in fear.

"This is our best chance at losing them." He performed a quick three-point turn with finesse the driver of the SUV did not possess. He kept the Jeep back far enough so that it wasn't visible from the road.

He withdrew his gun and reached for the door handle. Claire clutched his arm. "Are you going after them?"

He couldn't make out her features in the dim moonlight. It didn't matter. He didn't have to see her to know what she looked like. He had her face, her expressions, memorized. He knew she was staring at him with wide eyes. Her lips would be pressed into a frown. A worry line would be etched between her brows.

"I need to see which way they go." He gently pulled his arm from her grip. "I don't think there's any chance they saw us turn here. But if they did, I want to have the element of surprise."

Before she could launch a protest, he leaped out.

Staying close to the tree line, he ran to the road.

Dim headlights grew brighter by the second as the vehicle raced toward him. He moved into the foliage and crouched down. The SUV slowed as it reached the crossroads. Alex hoped it would turn but it rolled right through, speeding up again. He pressed himself against a tree, knowing his dark clothing would blend in.

The chances that the driver would realize this was the driveway he'd turned off on were slim. He was prepared regardless. They sped past. He squinted, hoping for a glimpse of the license plate. It was a fruitless attempt to gain information. It was too dark to make out anything. The vehicle continued on with no sign of slowing down.

He raced back to Claire. Flinging the door open, he slid inside.

"We lost them?" Claire demanded as they took off.

When they reached the edge of the driveway, taillights glowed red in the far distance.

"Looks that way."

Alex maneuvered onto the gravel road. He back-tracked to the crossroads their pursuers had avoided. He took a right, not sure where they were headed but not really caring. Once on this deserted stretch he flipped the headlights on.

He felt Claire's gaze burning into him.

"You have a lot of explaining to do," she said.

He shot her a wry look. "I could say the same for you."

# TWO

Claire read the description of the campground to Alex as he drove. Using his phone, she'd scanned several of them before finding one she thought might be a good fit.

"That one should work," he said as he flicked another glance into the rearview mirror.

Though they'd been driving without incident for half an hour now, she appreciated his vigilance.

"I think so, too," she agreed. "They accept dogs and it's less than an hour away, near the Tillamook State Forest." She read off the directions before sliding his smartphone into the Jeep's cup holder.

For weeks she had been fervently praying, asking God to help her. She had not anticipated help to arrive in the form of her ex-fiancé. Claire hadn't seen Alex in years. He'd left her at the worst possible time. He'd had no way of knowing she was pregnant with Mia. She hadn't figured it out herself until after he'd disappeared. She had no idea how he was going to react to finding out he had a daughter.

Having him barge back into her life was surreal. She kept sneaking glances, assuring herself it was really him.

Alex had spent years serving as an Army Ranger. After a mission gone horribly wrong, he had changed.

During his last deployment, a suicide bomber had blown up a school in an area he was supposed to be protecting. Men, women and far too many children had died. Though Claire had no doubt Alex had done everything by the book, he still blamed himself.

When he was discharged, he'd taken a job with an elite security company. It seemed to Claire he'd always put himself in harm's way. It was more than being an adrenaline junkie. It was as though he'd thought he could make up for the past if he pushed himself hard enough.

The problem was, no matter what he did, no matter how many lives he saved, it was never enough. He could never get over the lives that had been lost.

He'd fallen into a pit of self-loathing and despair. No matter how Claire had tried, she hadn't been able to help him. She hadn't been able to save Alex from himself, nor had she been able to save their relationship. Claiming she was better off without him, he'd walked away from her, from the plans they'd made, and he'd never looked back. Years ago she'd come to terms with the realization that she might never see him again. That's why his unexpected appearance was so hard to grasp.

Now that they had a plan of action for the night, she was ready to get some answers.

"How does Beth play into this?" she demanded. How had her sister been able to find him when Claire had spent *months* searching for Alex? Granted, that was years ago. At the time she'd exhausted every resource she had. Alex had been nowhere to be found. Emotionally drained and heartbroken, she'd given up the search and hadn't picked it up again. "I can't believe she was able to find you."

"She didn't find me. I contacted her."

After a moment of stunned silence she asked, "Why would you do that?"

"I came in on an international flight this morning. As I was walking through the airport I saw your face on a television screen." He cast a glance her way. "I stopped to listen to the news report. There aren't a lot of things that shock me these days, but that report was definitely one of them. I went home, did some quick research and realized you were in way over your head."

She couldn't argue. She needed help. If Alex was offering, it would be stupid and prideful to refuse. As much as seeing him had thrown her, she knew that if anyone could help her, it would be him.

"There's a warrant out for your arrest, you're on the run and the media is pushing the idea you crossed the border into Canada," he said, his tone matter of fact.

She turned to study his profile, barely illuminated by the dashboard lights. Earlier, when demanding the key, he'd said Claire was framed. "I didn't kill Jared."

"I know you didn't." His voice was calm and steady.

*She* knew that. She had been surprised to hear him say it.

"How do you know?" she demanded.

Alex held her gaze in his for a few silent heartbeats before returning his attention to the road. "We were together for a few years, Claire. Like it or not, I know you better than just about anyone. You couldn't have killed your husband, or anyone else for that matter. You don't have it in you. I saw you whip the gun into the trees at the shack. You'd rather risk your life than use it to defend yourself." He gave her another pointed look.

She turned from him, unable to bear the intensity of his stare. Closing her eyes, she leaned her head against the seat. Alex believed her. Beth believed her. Her sister hadn't hesitated in taking Mia, so Claire could work at proving her innocence. Maybe the rest of the world was against her, but knowing she had two people on her side gave her strength.

"I called Beth to ask if there was anything I could do to help," he continued. "She told me that you were framed. She said you were on the run, trying to gather evidence against the real murderer. She was on a roll and kept talking."

Claire wasn't surprised. Beth had probably known she'd had to take advantage of Alex's attention while she'd had it. Otherwise he might drop off the face of the world again, disappearing for another three years or more.

"She said you were hiding from a powerful man." His tone hardened. "She insisted your life was in danger. Then she told me about the shack, location and all. Beth said she wasn't positive that's where you'd gone, but she suspected."

"I didn't tell her," Claire said, "because I knew there was a warrant out for my arrest. I didn't want her involved any more than she had to be. I was sure the police would question her. I didn't want her to lie. Suspecting and knowing are very different things."

The hunting shack had belonged to their grandfather. He'd sold it over a decade ago to the couple who owned the adjoining land. They'd wanted to increase their acreage but had no interest in the shack. The building was rundown, and hadn't been used in years. When Claire had first arrived, it had been a mess. She'd cleaned it as best she could and turned it into a place of refuge.

"When we were kids, we used to say that if we ever ran away from home, that's where we'd go. I couldn't flat-out tell her that's where I was headed, but I was fairly certain she would figure it out."

"I get it." Alex tapped his fingers against the steering wheel.

"I thought it was an incredibly strange coincidence that Xavier's men found me the same time you did." She paused, cringing. "It wasn't a coincidence at all, was it?"

"Beth told me this guy was desperate to track you down and would probably go to any means necessary. If that's the case, and he seems to have plenty of resources at his disposal, I started to wonder if the phone line had been tapped," he admitted. "As soon as we hung up, I hit the road. I'd already learned what I could about the murder. Beth was adamant you'd been framed. She said she was sure these men were after you. Obviously she was right."

She frowned as she turned to face him again. "How did you get there so quickly?"

He hesitated, and she instinctively knew he didn't want to answer her question.

"I live right outside of Portland."

"Portland." Her voice was flat. For years she'd feared he was dead. "You still live in the area."

He stared straight ahead. "I have an apartment. I'm not there much. My work takes me all over the country. Sometimes out of the country."

She was quiet a moment, wrapping her head around that. She wasn't sure what "work" he was referring to these days, but she had to assume it was something dangerous. She also assumed he wouldn't answer if she asked, so she saved herself the trouble and kept her mouth shut. Even when they were engaged, much of Alex's professional life had been on a need-to-know basis. He'd more often than not decide she did not need to know.

He'd been in the business of saving people and, often times, discretion was key.

Claire shook her head. "I get it now. The reason you came after me today."

Alex gave her a wary look.

"You always have to save the world, be the hero. This," she said sadly as she tossed her hands in the air, "is what it takes. My life has to be in danger in order for me to finally have your attention."

"Claire," he said wearily, "it's not like that."

"Isn't it?" She was hit with a crushing wave of sadness. She had always admired Alex's selflessness. But at some point he'd taken it too far. His sole purpose in life had become trying to save strangers while distancing himself from those who were closest to him.

He didn't respond, and she didn't press the matter.

They rode in silence for a while, putting distance between them and Xavier's men.

"For what it's worth," he eventually said, "I'm sorry about your husband."

"I'm the first to admit it was not a happy marriage." She struggled to keep her voice steady. She had realized too late what a volatile temper Jared had had, how controlling he would be, how demeaning. "I'm relieved to be free of him, but I certainly didn't want him dead."

It pained her to admit it, but it was the truth. It was not something she wanted to talk to Alex about. She wasn't willing to divulge the details to him. Not yet. Maybe not ever.

"That's not how the media is spinning it." His words were a fact, not an accusation. "They're claiming your rocky marriage gave you the perfect motive for murder."

"I'm sure I can thank Xavier Ambrose for that."

"Jared's business partner."

"You did do your research."

"As much as I had time for." He cleared his throat and

Claire braced herself. There was so much history between them. There were so many hurts, so many things left unsaid. If Alex had looked into her life at all, he had to know about Mia. "Beth mentioned you left your daughter with her."

She was sure she didn't imagine the way his voice hitched ever so slightly on "daughter." With clenched fists, she waited for a barrage of questions. Silence hung heavy and cloying in the cab of the Jeep for several long, drawn-out heartbeats.

Minimal research would easily have uncovered that Mia was almost one by the time Claire and Jared had met. She was two by the time they'd married. She realized Alex wasn't ready to discuss Mia yet. Neither was she.

"I should let you know I sent a friend of mine to Beth's house. Gretchen looks harmless, but the woman is lethal."

"'Friend'?" Claire echoed. How close of a friend? Was Alex in a relationship? Had he found someone else to love after he'd told her his work had to come first? The thought sent a stab of pain through her heart. It wasn't jealousy she felt, she assured herself, but rather the old hurt. The realization that she wasn't enough for him.

Had Gretchen gotten through to him in a way she hadn't been able to?

"Colleague." He shot a look her way. "She's a colleague, and I trust her to keep them safe."

"Right." Claire fidgeted with the hem of her cardigan as worry began to niggle at her. "Beth lives in a gated community and her house has a top-notch security system. Do you think they could be in danger?"

Leaving her daughter behind had been the hardest thing she'd ever done. She'd only been able to go through with it because she'd been so sure that Mia would be completely safe with Beth. Far safer than if Claire had taken Mia on the run with her.

"Gretchen will check over Beth's security system, make sure it's up to par. I asked her to stay with Beth and her husband until this is over. I don't think your sister will fight her on it. She sounded frazzled when we spoke."

"I thought Mia would be safe with Beth," Claire admitted. "Wouldn't it be foolish of Xavier to go after her? It would draw unwanted attention to him, to the situation. He's framed me, wants me to look guilty. If something happened to Mia, it would be too suspicious. Do you think I was wrong? You never answered my question. Do you think they could be in danger?"

"You're probably right and Mia is probably safest with Beth," he agreed. "If he were to go after Mia, if she were harmed in any way, it would bring the investigation to a whole new level. Given how reporters are covering this story, something like that would cause a media explosion. But I've seen desperate people go to desperate measures. I prefer to err on the side of caution."

Claire's stomach clenched at the thought of anything happening to her daughter.

"Thank you. I appreciate the extra protection for my family. I'm sure Beth will, too," she said. Her sister was married to a cardiologist. Though Steven was brilliant, he was in the business of saving lives via complicated surgeries. Not protecting them by fending off gunmen.

She missed Mia so much her heart ached with it. Prior to this ordeal, she'd never spent a night away from her. Beth had always been actively involved in Mia's life. Claire knew Mia would be comfortable with Auntie Beth. Yet the child had to be confused. Claire didn't want her daughter to feel abandoned. She knew all too well how much it hurt to be left behind.

"Claire?"

Her head snapped up.

He motioned to a sign up ahead. "We're here."

Tourist season was over for the year. The small campground was nearly deserted. It was the perfect, indiscriminate place to stay. A Place in the Pines offered small, one-bedroom cabins in addition to its nearly empty campsites. The setting was rundown—or rustic—depending upon your perspective.

Alex scanned the parking lot as he returned to the Jeep. He was confident they hadn't been followed. He'd driven the back roads long enough to be sure they hadn't had a tail. Claire had not seemed happy with the prospect of spending time with him. Yet she hadn't argued, confirming just how afraid, how desperate, she was.

After what he'd put her through years ago, he owed her and he was going to take care of her now, the way he should've done back then.

His mind was still reeling, trying to come to terms with what he'd inadvertently uncovered earlier in the day. He had a child. Though the online article he'd read hadn't mentioned him by name, he was sure of it. It stated that Claire had a three-year-old daughter from a previous relationship. It didn't take a mathematician to figure that one out. The fact was driven home when the article stated that the girl's father had been absent from her life.

At the time, he thought he had good reason for leaving. Now he wasn't so sure.

Regret stabbed at him when he remembered how difficult he'd been. How withdrawn. He'd been plagued by nightmares, riddled with guilt over what had happened overseas. How could he ever make Claire understand that pushing himself, going to the extreme, had been the only way to quiet those feelings? It had worked, but only for a while. The guilt always came back with a vengeance. It wasn't until after he'd found a connection with God a couple years ago that he'd been able to find peace within himself. It had taken being jumped in a dark, grungy alley and nearly losing his life to get to that place.

Now he did his job for the right reason. He was no longer running from the past but living for every moment when he could reconnect a person with their loved ones. Sure, his job was still dangerous, but he was good at it. He was cautious now in a way he hadn't been back then.

He'd returned from breaking up a human trafficking ring just this morning. Now he wished he'd returned weeks ago. He could've been helping Claire all along. Helping her with what, exactly, he wasn't sure yet. He was going to find out. She'd mentioned Xavier Ambrose a few times now.

While reading about the murder of Jared Mitchell, Xavier's name had come up several times. They were business partners who owned a successful hotel chain.

The media suggested a volatile marriage between Claire and Jared. His gut instinct kicked in. *Claire* and *volatile* were not words that belonged in the same sentence. If their marriage was truly volatile, he had no doubt Jared was to blame.

Alex felt a surge of anger. His mind took off with scenarios he didn't want to think of. If Jared had hurt her…

He pushed out a breath. If Jared had hurt her, he would face judgment with the Lord for that. There was nothing Alex could do. Especially not now that Jared was dead.

He reached the Jeep and hopped inside.

"Do we have a place to stay?"

"We do." He held up the key. Claire's face was plastered on newspapers, the television, the internet. They both knew she had to stay out of sight as much as possible. "It's the one on the end."

He drove the short distance to the last cabin in a row of five. All were painted the same deep brown with green shutters. Only one cabin in the middle had a car parked in front of it.

"Tomorrow morning we'll have to run into town," he said. "I'll need a couple changes of clothes. I had a duffel bag in the vehicle I left behind, but we're obviously not going back there." He tapped the backpack she clutched on her lap. "Do you have enough to get by?"

"I should."

"Let's get you into the cabin." He got out, pulling the seat forward. Roscoe dropped to the ground with a grunt. His stubby tail wagged as he scoped out their new surroundings.

Claire clutched her backpack as she followed.

Alex quickly opened the door, flipped on the light and ushered Claire in.

The cabin was sparsely decorated but appeared to be clean. When he went into town for clothes, he'd have to grab some groceries, as well. There was no telling how long they would be there.

"It's not exactly paradise," he said to Claire, "but it'll have to do."

She gave him a cool look. "Compared to where I've been staying, it is paradise. At least it has running water."

"How did you get by in that shack?" Alex asked.

"I took the Jeep into town a few times a week. There's a truck stop that has showers. I had a propane cookstove, water jugs, a cooler. I made it work." She moved into the cabin, placing her backpack on the table.

"You went into town and no one recognized you?"

"I was careful."

"How careful?" It seemed like an awfully big risk to take. She had told him a bit about the Jeep. He already knew she'd purchased the Jeep it in cash from an old farmer. She hadn't changed the title card on it and the thing didn't have insurance.

They should ditch it as soon as they had the chance. Not only was it illegal to drive, but Xavier's men had seen it. They'd be on the lookout for it.

"I wore a disguise every time I went to town." She frowned. "I had no choice. I needed an internet connection. I used the connection at the local library. They had chairs scattered all over the upper level. I could charge my laptop and research at the same time. No one paid any attention to me."

"Care to tell me what you were researching?"

"I can do better than that. I'll show you."

She tugged the backpack's zipper down. Reaching in, she pulled out a black binder. "Xavier Ambrose killed Jared. Unfortunately, I don't have enough evidence to prove it."

She handed the binder to him.

"Tell me what you need from me."

A sharp laugh cut through the cabin. "What I *need* from you?"

He realized that could be a loaded question. Or maybe not. She was looking at him as though the only thing she needed was for him to go away.

"You need help," he said firmly. "That's obvious." He offered up a small smile. "Though I have to admit, seeing you take down two men with nothing but pepper spray was a pretty amazing sight. You must've used the good stuff. Police grade."

He knew the stickier spray wouldn't blow back in the sprayer's face. The heat of the red pepper spray would be debilitating. Because it was a gel, it was harder to clean off. She had made a good choice.

"I didn't take them down with just pepper spray," Claire corrected, "I took them down with Roscoe's help. Without him startling them the way he did, I think the outcome would've been very different."

He couldn't argue with that.

"Read through that information and tell me what you think," Claire requested. "That's all I need from you right now."

He clenched the binder in his hand.

Roscoe whined as he leaned against Claire's leg.

Alex knew he was being ridiculous, but he felt as if Roscoe was holding a grudge. Though Claire was too panicked to realize it was Alex coming out of the woods at the shack, he was pretty sure Roscoe had known. The dog had stuck by Claire's side, not acknowledging Alex until he'd commanded the dog's attention. Even now, Roscoe was making it clear who his real owner was.

Alex couldn't blame him. He'd abandoned the dog, as well. It didn't seem to matter that Alex had spent countless hours working with Roscoe, turning him into the disciplined animal he was today. They'd spent many afternoons going for jogs or playing fetch. But in the end, the dog had become Claire's, and Claire's alone.

"I should take him out," she said.

"I'll do it. I'm not having you walk around out there in the dark."

"You said there was no chance we were followed."

"I stand by that."

"Then what do you care if I'm outside, alone in the dark?" She wrapped her arms around her slender waist.

He heard the challenge in her words and sighed.

"Look, Claire, I don't want to fight with you. I think

we've done enough of that to last a lifetime." He raked his free hand through his hair. He wanted to ask her about Mia, but one look at Claire, so on edge, warned him it wasn't a good time. He couldn't imagine the conversation going well right now. So, he'd wait. Instead he asked, "Can we call a truce? Can we concentrate on the current problem instead of getting bogged down by the problems of the past?"

"Yes. I'm sorry." Her shoulders drooped, and she seemed to deflate in front of him. "I'm not myself these days. I'm exhausted. I'm terrified I'm going to spend the rest of my life in prison, paying for a crime I didn't commit."

"That's not going to happen. I won't let it." It was a promise he intended to keep. "You're not on your own anymore. I'm going to help you figure this out."

And if he didn't? If they couldn't find the proof she needed? He had a backup plan. He'd get her and their daughter out of the country. He had the resources to do it. He wouldn't allow her to be sent to prison when he knew she was innocent. And then…well, he couldn't let himself think too far ahead. His mind was still reeling from what he'd discovered earlier in the day. He and Claire needed to have a serious talk about the little girl staying with Beth.

Soon.

Just not quite yet because, despite how anxious he was for answers, Claire looked as if she were about ready to collapse from exhaustion.

"Thank you." Her words were a breathy whisper. "I don't think I've said that yet."

"You don't need to thank me."

"I do. Even though you're standing right here, I'm having a hard time grasping the fact that you came after me." Her lower lip trembled as he watched her fight for composure. "I was so sure I'd never see you again."

Did she really think so little of him that it surprised her that he was there to help? She probably did. Worse yet, he probably deserved it. When he'd walked out on her, he had been in a bad place emotionally. He'd thought he was doing the right thing. He'd been sure cutting her free was the kindest thing to do. She'd deserved better than to be tied to a man who was so miserable to be around.

Maybe he'd been wrong.

He didn't know.

"I'll never be able to tell you how sorry I am about the way I ended things," he admitted.

She studied his face for a moment, looked as if she wanted to say something and then forced a weak smile. "You were right. My current problem is big enough. It would be silly to drag up problems from the past."

Roscoe released a loud, theatrical whine. He didn't appreciate being kept waiting. Alex reached for the doorknob, ready to let the dog out, but twisted back around when Claire spoke again.

"I'm just happy to know you're alive and well," Claire said. "I prayed for you. Every night. I prayed for your safety and for healing." She dropped her gaze, unable to look him in the eye. "I pray for you still."

"I didn't know you were the praying type," he said, feeling somewhat surprised. Maybe he didn't know Claire as well as he thought he did.

"Things change." She lifted her chin. "After you left, Beth convinced me to start attending church with her. A lot of years had passed since I'd stepped foot inside a chapel. Once I did—" she gave a small shrug "—it made me question why I ever let myself drift away from the church in the first place. I started reading my Bible again and I began to pray. I prayed a lot."

"God heard you," he said gently. "He heard you loud and clear. It took some time for me to listen to Him, but He finally helped me get my head straightened out."

Claire looked at him quizzically. "You're a Christian now?"

"Yes," he said firmly. "Maybe sometime I'll tell you how that came about. But it's a story better saved for another time."

She looked like she wanted to push the matter, but a yawn cut off her words.

It was for the best. Maybe sometime he'd tell her about the stabbing that had taken place in the alley. Maybe he'd tell her how it had changed his life. But he didn't want to get into that tonight. It was clear she had enough weighing on her and he didn't want to add to that.

"Get some sleep," Alex suggested as he motioned toward the bedroom. "I'll take the couch. You'll be safe here."

She shook her head. "You can think what you like, but until this is over, I won't be safe anywhere."

"Claire—" his tone was firm "—I won't let anyone hurt you."

She leveled him with a look that clearly stated he had already hurt her more than anyone else could.

"You're right," she said quietly. She picked up her bag, edging away from Alex as she headed toward the bedroom. "I should get some sleep. I'm tired. I can't deal with any more tonight."

He thought she probably meant she couldn't deal with *him* any more tonight. He couldn't blame her. He would help her clear her name. It wouldn't absolve him of his past mistakes, but it was something. Then he would allow her to get on with her life.

# THREE

Claire struggled to force her eyes open as she fought against the sensation of water filling her nose, her mouth, threatening to fill her lungs. Her limbs vibrated with anxiety as a feeling of dread flowed through her body. She tried to move but her arms felt weighted down, too heavy to budge.

She gasped for air as she willed herself out of the nightmare that had plagued her since Jared's death. She tried not to think of that awful day, but the memories consistently wound themselves into her dreams. Jared had drowned…and she'd nearly drowned trying to save him.

Blinking into the dimly lit room, she felt disoriented. Where was she?

She scrambled into a sitting position, heart hammering wildly. Hazy light crept through the sides of the curtains, barely offering enough light to see by. Unfamiliar walls surrounded her. A strange door was straight across from her. Panic sizzled through her veins as the foreign room came into focus. She jerked fully awake as she tried to get her bearings.

A soft nudge against her hand immediately calmed her. Roscoe whimpered, as if sensing her panic. He nudged her again, the action instantly setting her at ease. She let her hand drift over his head. His silky fur felt familiar and comforting under her palm.

She hated reliving the moment she'd found Jared face-down in the pool. She'd jumped in without thinking, her fleece bathrobe weighing her down, pulling her under, anchoring her below the surface. She'd struggled with the tie around her waist, fighting to get it undone so she could slip free. Once out of the robe, she'd broken the surface of the water, gasping for air even as she swam toward Jared. She'd dragged him to the edge, pulled him out. Her efforts had been in vain. He had died within moments of being shoved into the pool. The blow to his head incapacitating him enough that he'd dragged in a water-filled breath and that had been the end of him.

Her own lungs burned as she dropped back onto her pillow. She shoved the nightmarish memory aside. Other nightmarish memories quickly seeped in, filling her mind with another brand of terror as she thought of the harrowing evening she'd had.

She'd escaped Xavier's men by the grace of God, and the grace of God alone. She focused on that realization. God had been with her. He had protected her.

Eventually her heartbeat calmed to a dull, hollow thud.

She tried to tell herself she was safe but couldn't quite force herself to believe it.

On the other side of the door rested another sort of threat.

Alex would never ever hurt her physically. Not like Jared had. But the man was hazardous to her emotional state. Last night the shock of seeing him had numbed some of the hurt.

Roscoe ducked out from under her ministrations. He moved to the closed door and treated her to a pathetic look as he silently pleaded to be let outside.

Claire tossed off the blankets and swung her legs around the side of the bed. She shivered despite the comfy sweatshirt and sweatpants she'd slept in. Her body still tingled with the echoing fear of her nightmare. Would her life ever feel normal again?

The bedroom door creaked when she pulled it open.

Alex's blanket—an extra one she'd found in a dresser drawer—was already folded and tossed over the back of the couch. His pillow was neatly propped against the armrest. He stood before the window, his body alert, always ready for action.

Claire watched him for a moment. Mixed emotions swirled through her. He had left her. He left her alone. Scared. Pregnant. Grieving over the loss of her fiancé, her best friend.

Seeing him now, she couldn't help but think of what could have been. They should've been married by now. They should've been a family. Alex, her and Mia. If things had gone differently, would Mia have had a little brother or sister? She could so easily imagine Christmas mornings by the tree, church together every Sunday. Family dinners, Saturday morning breakfasts.

She shook the thoughts away. That had been her dream once. But Alex had killed that dream.

He turned to face her, a cardboard cup of coffee in one hand. His hair was damp and he was clean-shaven. Despite wearing yesterday's clothes, he managed to look put-together.

"The office carries a few essentials," he said. "There're powdered doughnuts on the table and a cup of coffee for you. I got Roscoe a couple packages of hot dogs. I know it's not ideal but it'll get us by for the morning. I got myself a razor, toothbrush, toothpaste. If you need anything, let me know and I'll go get it."

She nodded. "Thanks."

"I'll take him out so you can have a few minutes to yourself."

When he was gone she carefully rummaged around in her backpack. A toiletry bag held enough to get her by for a few more days. She had several outfits in there, more than one would have thought. Each rolled into a tight, efficient bundle. Each plain and perfunctory.

In a side, zippered pocket was her second bottle of pepper spray. Like the one she'd used at the cabin, it belonged on the end of a key chain. Instead she'd put it on the end of a cord so she could wear it around her neck. She didn't need it now but was grateful she had thought to buy more than one.

She grabbed what she needed and headed to the bathroom. By the time she got out of the shower, Roscoe was tended to, her coffee was cool and Alex looked apprehensive. An unusual look for him.

He patted the seat next to him at the table.

She dropped down into it, happily taking a doughnut. It was dried out, but she was ravenous. Even the lukewarm coffee was a treat. She was halfway through her coffee before she realized her wallet was open on the table. The plastic sleeve that held pictures was conspicuously absent.

Her last bite of doughnut tasted like chalk. She gulped some coffee to choke it down.

"I shouldn't have dug through your things," he admitted. "But I couldn't wait any longer. I assumed you had a picture of her." He held up the photos. "She's the prettiest little thing I've ever seen."

Claire met his eyes. His expression was guarded. Yet it was so like Alex to bluntly jump right into the conversation without preamble.

She appreciated his directness and intended to reciprocate.

"I need you to understand that I never wanted to keep Mia from you." Claire paused, taking a moment to organize her thoughts. "It took me a while to realize I was pregnant. I wasn't feeling well. I was sick for months. I attributed it to stress." She'd attributed it to a shattered heart. She saw no point in laying that accusation on him. "By the time I knew I was pregnant, I had no idea how to find you. I did try. You had been behaving so recklessly, as if you had no regard for your own life. Each mission you took was more dangerous than the last. I was afraid of what I would find. I was so afraid you'd been killed. I had to stop looking."

"I left the country for a while." He cleared his throat. "I'm in a better place now."

"I can tell." His eyes no longer held the haunted, hollow look. "I'm happy for you."

"I take full responsibility for how badly things ended with us." He raked a hand through his hair. "I should've faced my problems, worked on our relationship. But when I needed the most courage, I ran."

Claire felt all of her old arguments rising to the surface. He didn't need to run. She would stand by his side always. They could get through anything, if only he would let her in.

It was too late for all of that. Though it surprised her to hear him admit to his past mistakes, she couldn't get sidetracked by that right now.

She tamped down thoughts from the past, deciding to focus on the present.

"Does Gretchen know Mia is your daughter?"

"If she does, she figured it out on her own. At the time I sent her, I'd only known a few hours, having just run across an article stating you had a three-year-old daughter from a previous relationship. I was still grappling with the information and didn't feel I had the right to claim her as my own."

"And now?"

"Now that the shock has worn off, I want more than anything to meet my little girl." A muscle ticked in his jaw. "If that's okay with you."

She swallowed the lump of emotion rising in her throat. When she'd first found out she was pregnant, she'd tried to track Alex down. She had wanted nothing more than to be a family. But now, so much time had passed. They'd gone their separate ways, were living completely different lives. Yet Mia was still his daughter and she couldn't deny either of them the relationship they deserved. "We'll need to discuss some ground rules," she said firmly. "I don't want you flitting in and out of her life. It will only confuse her. She's been through enough. I won't allow you to hurt her."

"You think I'd hurt my own daughter?" Alex asked, his tone incredulous.

"Not intentionally, no," Claire said. "But if you disappoint her one too many times, if she realizes she can't count on you—"

"So what you're saying is that you don't think I can be a good father," Alex said, cutting her off.

"That's not what I said," Claire argued. "What I *am* saying is that to be a good parent you need to be present. You need to be involved."

His jaw clenched as he thought that over. "Look, I get where you're coming from," he finally said. "I understand why you might have concerns. But I *will* be a good dad."

Claire studied his face for a moment. His gaze was intense, his expression determined. In that moment she believed he *wanted* to be a good father, but he knew nothing of how demanding a young child could be. He didn't understand how one too many broken promises could lead to broken trust.

"Claire," he said, his tone softening, "I realize you don't have a lot of faith in me at this point. But if you let me, I'll make Mia a priority in my life."

Claire forced a smile, trying to ease some of the tension hanging over them. She wasn't necessarily persuaded by his words, but she needed to give Alex the chance to know his daughter, without her old hurts clouding her judgment. "We'll see." Her tone was clipped and she wasn't sure what more she could say right then. There would be time to figure it out later.

"You don't sound too convinced," he said in annoyance.

"I guess time will tell," Claire replied.

Alex nodded curtly. "Fair enough."

He glanced down at the photo he still held. Claire heard his breath catch. "She really is beautiful."

"She is," Claire said. "She has your eyes."

"She has your smile." Alex finally lifted his gaze to meet hers.

"You should have this." Claire took the plastic sleeve from him and slid one of Mia's photos from it. She'd looked at it so many times she had it memorized. "It seems only fair that I should share."

Alex didn't argue, confirming Claire's suspicion that he wanted it badly.

"Thank you." He gave it a long, hard look before taking out his wallet and sliding it inside.

"The sooner we get your name cleared, the sooner I can meet my daughter," Alex said. His heartbeat sped up at the thought. There had been a time when he couldn't wait to start a family with Claire. That dream had vanished like vapor when he'd allowed his past to own him. Yesterday, when he'd run across the article mentioning Mia, he'd had to reread the line countless times before the words made sense. Even now, he wasn't sure the news had completely sunk in.

A full day later and it still seemed so surreal.

He fought to tamp down the frustration he felt. He wanted to tell Claire that he wasn't the person he used to be. Like her, he'd found a connection with the Lord and it had changed him. He didn't want to see the look of doubt in her eyes. He was pretty sure she wished just about anyone else had come to her rescue. He'd be lying if he said that didn't hurt, at least a little.

"Did you look through the information I gave you?" Claire asked, pulling him from his thoughts.

"I did." He was impressed. She had compiled detailed information regarding sales made by Xavier. She had buyers' names, dates of sales, pickup sites and purchase prices. "You've built a very good case against Xavier. I don't think there's any disputing he's fencing stolen antiquities. Why haven't you taken this to the police?"

"Does anything in that file prove he murdered Jared?"

He frowned. "No."

"Exactly. Having *him* locked up for fraud wouldn't get *me* off the hook for murder." She fidgeted with her coffee cup. "I was hoping to tie him to Jared's death using the information in the file I gave you. I haven't been able to do that yet."

"You've compiled a lot of information on the antiques Xavier was fencing," Alex said. "How were you able to get the documentation?"

"Jared." She winced. "I took most of it from him."

"He was involved?"

"Yes. It's what got him killed."

Alex could use another cup of coffee, but he wasn't about to walk away from this conversation, not even for a minute.

"In order for me to help you, I need the whole story. Can you start from the beginning? You need to tell me everything."

"'The beginning'?" she echoed.

Claire was strong and determined, always had been. Now she seemed hardened, world-weary. It was a burden Alex was familiar with and never wanted Claire to have to carry. She'd always been welcoming, open, quick to smile. Now she seemed closed off, cynical.

"I'm supposed to tell *you* all about how awful my marriage was?" She squeezed her eyes closed and pinched the bridge of her nose.

She looked defeated as she slumped into her chair. If there was a way he could spare her from this, he would. But if he was going to help, he needed the facts. All of them.

"I am at fault somewhat," she said. "I rushed into the marriage. After you left, I was angry. I was hurt. I was missing you terribly. I had a new baby and I didn't want to be alone. Jared was charming. He treated me well at first." She picked up her coffee cup, realized it was empty and set it back down. "Looking back, I realize he was too charming. Too perfect. But after we were married that changed. I have no doubt he wanted a wife because it fit the image he was trying to create. His investors were more comfortable with a family man. Many of them saw him as altruistic, taking in a child that wasn't his own. He doted on Mia in public, putting on a wonderful show, as always. But in private, he ignored her. It was probably for the best, but it was very confusing for Mia."

Thinking of another man raising his daughter was like an emotional sucker punch to the heart. So much had changed in the past twenty-four hours. He was still trying to comprehend that he had a daughter. Not just the fact that he had a daughter but all the emotional turmoil that entailed, including having abandoned her. Having missed out on three entire years of her precious, young life.

"He treated her okay?"

"He never hurt her, if that's what you're asking."

It was. He pushed ahead with the next question. "And you? Did he hurt you?"

"We weren't married long before I realized he wasn't the man I thought he was. I knew he was a man of power. I didn't realize he was a man of unscrupulous morals. Looking back, I wonder if I missed the signs. Or maybe there were no signs. He hid his dark side from the world. When we met, he hid it from me. Once we were married, it emerged. It came out swinging, quite literally," she murmured.

"Why didn't you leave him?" Alex asked as he struggled to keep his voice even.

"I tried to leave him once. It didn't end well," she said quietly. "He threatened to take Mia from me if I filed for divorce. He had no claim to her, but I couldn't risk it. I couldn't risk him winning even partial custody because he would've only done so out of spite. With high-powered lawyers and bottomless pockets, I was afraid he could pull it off. I wouldn't have put it past him to pay off the judge. I knew if I was going to try to leave him again, I had to be able to remove myself from his reach."

"How did you plan to do that?" Alex asked. "Get out of his reach, I mean."

"Last spring we had Xavier over for dinner. I went upstairs to put Mia to bed. When I came back down the two of them were in Jared's office arguing. Jared told Xavier he knew all about his 'special endeavor.' That's what he called it. It piqued my interest and I couldn't get my feet to move. I knew it was a conversation I shouldn't overhear, but I couldn't stop myself."

Alex nodded, indicating he was following.

"At the time I didn't realize they were talking about the black market. However, Jared made a comment that stuck with me. He said he had proof Xavier terminated those who got in his way." She forced a bitter laugh. "I thought 'terminated' meant he fired them. I'm so naïve. I'm still having a hard time wrapping my mind around the fact that there are people in the world evil enough to kill someone over a business deal."

"Is that what happened with Jared? He got in Xavier's way and was going to turn him in?"

"No," Claire scoffed. "Oh, no. Jared didn't have the moral aptitude for that. He used the information to threaten Xavier. He didn't want to shut the operation down, he wanted in on the action. He was using what he knew to blackmail Xavier into cutting him in on the deals. Xavier didn't want to share. *That's* what got Jared killed."

Claire's words hung in the air as Alex took a moment to think over everything she'd told him.

"That night, Xavier agreed to Jared's demands. I knew they were talking about some sort of illegal activity, I just didn't know *what*. Jared was gone a lot, checking out potential locations for new hotels. He was careless with his files because as far as he knew, I had no reason to be digging. It didn't take me long to realize they were fencing antiquities on the black market.

"I started making copies of everything I found. I had every intention of taking it to the police. I knew if I could get Jared locked up, it would provide me the chance to escape." She shook her head. "I waited too long, wanting to be *sure* my proof was solid enough. I knew the two of them would hire the best lawyers. I wanted to be rid of Jared. I didn't want to take the chance of them getting off. Xavier has less patience and isn't the sort of man to tolerate being blackmailed. He took Jared down and set me up."

Alex patted the black file. "This is the information Jared was using against Xavier?"

"Part of it. I think there has to be more, but I've been unable to find it. As soon as it was determined Jared was murdered, the police confiscated his computer." She offered a small shrug. "I don't think they'll find much on it. I never did. I think he was afraid if he stored information on the hard drive, Xavier would find a way to hack into his system. The files in the binder are off a Jumpdrive."

"Where is the Jumpdrive now?" Alex asked.

Claire shook her head and shrugged. "I don't know. About a week before he was killed, it disappeared. He'd been keeping it in his desk drawer. Maybe he realized I was onto him."

"You don't think the information you have is enough to put Xavier away?"

"At this point, he could claim Jared was the front man. What if Xavier walks? It would be like kicking a hornets' nest."

"He's already after you."

"I thought he only wanted to frame me." She pulled in a breath. "After your phone call with Beth, he knows I'm onto him. If her line really was tapped—and judging by the appearance of the men last night, it seems likely—he would've heard her say I knew I was framed, that I was searching for evidence. I don't think framing me is enough anymore. I think he wants me dead. If he knows I'm looking for evidence, he'll do anything in his power to stop me."

Alex knew she wasn't exaggerating. The gunmen at the cabin attested to that.

"What's your game plan?" he asked. "You said you've been doing research the past few weeks. What are you looking into?"

"It goes back to that first conversation. I thought jobs were on the line. I didn't realize lives were on the line." Her fingers tapped listlessly against her thighs. "Jared said Xavier terminated someone who got in his way. *Terminated.* Past tense."

"Meaning it wasn't a threat, but something he'd already carried out."

"Yes." Claire frowned. "I've looked up every name in this file."

"You only have a list of buyers."

"Right."

"Any of them dead?" The question was blunt but necessary.

"No."

"So chances are," Alex said as he thought it over, "if Xavier took someone else out, it was a middle man. Maybe someone in charge of sales."

"That's what I'm thinking," Claire agreed. "Maybe even a competitor. He probably made it look like an accident."

"Like he tried to do with Jared?"

A grim look settled on Claire's face. "That was the initial report. Jared had a gash on the back of his head. I assumed he'd tripped and hit his head on the edge of the pool. When the emergency responders first arrived, they seemed to think so, too. However the autopsy showed there were flecks of paint in the gash. They matched the paint on a lawn statue in our backyard. Whoever killed Jared hit him with the statue before shoving him into the pool. His official cause of death was drowning."

"But whoever hit him over the head wanted him dead," Alex finished. "Did they find the statue?"

"The statue was in the garden where it had always been. There were still traces of blood when the investigators came back."

"No fingerprints?"

She winced. "Only mine. It's my flower garden."

"How convenient," Alex said sourly. "That's when you became a suspect?"

She nodded. "I was brought in for questioning, but they let me go. I already had my suspicions by then. As soon as I knew Jared had been murdered, I knew Xavier was involved. They questioned him, as well. He told them Jared and I had a troubled marriage. Things went sideways pretty quickly from there."

"You didn't tell them you suspected Xavier?" Alex asked.

"Of course I did," Claire said. "But I don't think they took my suspicion seriously. One of the detectives asked if I was accusing Xavier out of retaliation because of what he'd said about my marriage to Jared. The information I have regarding the antiquities just as easily points to Jared being the front man. I have no proof that Xavier was dabbling in the black market, let alone that he's a murderer.

"When I left the station that afternoon, they told me not to leave town."

"So that's exactly what you did." Alex shook his head.

"That doesn't sound like the Claire I knew. You've always been a rule follower."

Her spine stiffened, and she sat straighter. "That's because the Claire you knew didn't have a daughter to protect. She's already growing up without her father. I'm not going to allow her to grow up without her mother."

"Keep that attitude," Alex said, refusing to take offense at her words because he knew she didn't mean for him to. "I have a feeling you're going to need it."

"What I *need*," Claire said firmly, "is to prove that Xavier really did have someone killed and that Jared knew it. That would give him motive to keep Jared quiet. Permanently."

"You hit dead ends with the names in the file," Alex said.

"True. But I know someone who might know something."

"Yeah?" Alex raised an eyebrow. "Who would that be?"

"Ruth Crenshaw. She was Jared's secretary. She left a message saying she needed to speak with me. Her message wasn't detailed but she did say she had information about Jared that could be important," Claire said. "By the time I got the chance to contact her, she was gone."

"Gone?"

"She left A & M Inc. after Jared's funeral. It makes sense. Jared was her boss. Though, to be honest, I think there was more to it than that. She was afraid when she left the message. I could hear it in her voice."

"How do you know she's no longer at A & M?"

"After I left, I tried getting in touch with her. I was told she no longer worked there. I asked where she'd gone but I was told they couldn't give out that information. I found her home phone number but it was disconnected."

"Do you know where she lives?" Alex asked. He was already reaching for his phone.

"No. Her address wasn't listed."

"Give me a few minutes. I'm sure I can figure it out."

# FOUR

Claire's short, newly darkened hair was scrunched into waves. She wore a gray knit cap and chunky glasses. Her makeup was light, an artfully drawn beauty mark etched over her upper lip. With her leggings, black turtleneck and blue flannel shirt wrapped around her waist, she looked like a college student. Like any one of a hundred or more chic hipsters that could be found in any Portland coffee shop.

In addition to her subtle disguise, she'd lost weight. Her face was gaunt, making her cheekbones more prominent. Alex would know her anywhere, but for the rest of the world, it was an excellent disguise.

He was hit with a feeling of nostalgia. He'd loved this woman so deeply once. He knew he would always care for Claire. Knowing they had a daughter together bonded them forever. If things were different, he could almost imagine marrying her, becoming a family. It frustrated him that she didn't think he could be a good father. And if she had her doubts about that, anything more would certainly not sit well with her. He mentally pushed the thoughts aside. There was no sense going there. The time for that had passed.

He'd blown any chance of a relationship with his past

mistakes. Now all he could do was try to make up for walking away like he had. He'd help Claire out of this mess and, as soon as he was able, he'd prove to her he could be a great dad.

For now he had to settle for helping her track down her best lead.

As much as he disliked Claire being out in the open, he disliked the idea of leaving her behind even more. He was confident that she would not be recognized as they drove into the city to begin their search for Ruth.

They were almost to Ruth's neighborhood when his cell phone rang. It was a new phone, different from the one he'd used when speaking with Beth, and very few people had the number.

He felt Claire's concern as he listened to the man on the other end. The conversation was quick, to the point, and really not all that surprising.

"What's wrong?" Claire asked when he disconnected.

"That was the driver of the tow truck." He'd called a company earlier in the morning to make arrangements to have his vehicle brought to the nearest town. He didn't want to risk meeting up with Xavier's men by fetching it himself. He had no reason to believe they'd cause any trouble for a towing company. "He got my truck back to their shop but he wanted to let me know it's been heavily vandalized. Xavier's men broke all the windows."

"They wanted to search inside."

"That's my guess," he agreed. "They won't find any-thing. They can use my license plate number to trace the vehicle back to me. At this point I don't think it really matters. I'm sure they figured out who I am right after the phone call with Beth."

Claire winced. "I'm sorry you got dragged into this."

nd time. It was nothing like the decked-out SUV
ier's men had driven the other day, but maybe the
 had gotten smarter. Alex didn't get a good look at
guy behind the wheel. His features were hidden by a
eball cap and a pair of trendy sunglasses.

"I couldn't tell you that, either." The woman laughed
f-consciously. "I'm sorry. I realize I'm no help at all."

Alex pulled his attention away from the street. He
rced a quick smile. "Thanks, anyway. I appreciate your
me."

If not for the sedan, Alex would've checked in with
ther neighbors. He wasn't going to risk it today. He
gged back to the Jeep.

Claire had climbed into the driver's seat. She fired up
he engine when she saw him heading her way. He wasn't
bout to argue with her.

"That car's gone past twice." Claire turned around in
uth's driveway. "I tried to get a license number but the
late was covered in mud."

Alex was on high alert as Claire drove. He'd already
id his Glock from his holster. He hated the idea of using
in a residential area. As the car did a U-turn, he hoped
wouldn't come to that.

"Maybe he's just lost."

"Maybe." Alex wasn't entirely convinced and could
 by her tone that Claire wasn't, either. Following the
ed limit, she cruised out of the neighborhood. With
ire behind the wheel, it allowed Alex to be more vig-
t. He watched over his shoulder as the sedan turned

Turn left at the intersection up here. He turned off
e could be trying to cut us off up ahead."
aire did as directed.

"Don't be. I'm not. It's not as if they're going to take
the information to the police. They're not going to want
to explain what they were doing out at the hunting shack,
or how they know I'm involved."

"I'm also sorry about the damage."

"That's what insurance is for."

Thoughts of insurance reminded him he needed to be
extra cautious while driving the Jeep. He wasn't going to
do anything that would result in being pulled over. The
lack of registration and insurance ate at him, but there
wasn't much he could do about it just yet. He'd contemplated a rental car but was leery of it being traced. He
also knew showing up at the campground with a new
vehicle would draw unwanted attention.

For now, though he didn't like it, the Jeep was their
only option.

"Do you know Ruth well?" Alex wondered.

He had found an address for her in a middle-class
neighborhood on the edge of Portland.

"We were friendly," Claire said. "She worked at the
desk in the lobby of A & M Inc. She was the first face
you saw when you walked in the door. I didn't visit Jared
at work often but when I did, I always stopped to chat
with Ruth."

"You're on good terms?"

"I believe so." Claire's eyebrows scrunched in thought.
"She's an older woman, nearing retirement age. Her husband passed away—massive stroke—a few years ago. I
volunteered to help with the luncheon at the church after
the funeral. She was so grateful. When Jared died, she
sent a beautiful bouquet and such a lovely card."

Alex checked the street sign up ahead. "We're almost
there." He turned into the residential area. Claire had

switched out the hipster glasses for a pair of sunglasses he'd gotten at a gas station.

He had his own cheap pair perched on his nose.

"That's it," Claire said, sounding slightly distressed. She rattled off the street number just to be sure she was looking at the right house. "It looks like this lead just died."

Alex parked a few houses down from the white bungalow with a For Sale sign in the front yard.

"Not necessarily," he said. "She might still be living here. I'm going to see if anyone is home."

Roscoe poked his head between their seats. His ears perked up when he heard the door handle engage.

"Stay!" Alex commanded.

He dropped back to the floor.

"Be careful," Claire ordered.

He appreciated the way she was scanning the street. He didn't think they'd been followed, didn't think anyone would bother looking for them there, but knew you could never be too cautious.

School was out for the day. Several houses down, a father was playing catch with his son and daughter. The sight of them made Alex smile. In the other direction, a woman was weeding her flower bed. Someone in the neighborhood had lit a charcoal grill. The scent wafted through the air as he strode up Ruth's sidewalk.

He pushed the doorbell, stepped aside and waited. From this angle he was still able to keep an eye on the street. Traffic was light as people began coming home from work, and Alex watched as a beige car drove by. He stabbed at the doorbell again. It was possible Ruth was working late. He thought they'd given her plenty of time to get home.

But maybe not.

Or maybe she had errands to run.

The woman weeding her flowers kept g

He smiled and gave her a nod.

Brushing the dirt off her gardening glo back.

Alex knew it would be a wasted effor doorbell a third time.

He clomped down the cement steps and cu neighbor's yard.

"Good afternoon," he called.

"Hello." The woman rose to her feet. "You'r for Ruth, I assume?"

"I am," Alex agreed. "We have a mutual frien pen to be passing through town, thought I'd s say hello. Do you happen to know if she typicall late? I'm wondering if I should stick around for a

"That would be a waste of your time." The gave him an apologetic shrug. "She moved ou weeks ago. I didn't see her, but a moving van don't know where she moved to."

"That's unfortunate. My friend will be bur wasn't able to connect with her." Alex didn't fake the disappointment in his voice. "I know to work at A & M Inc. I heard she left there. Do pen to know where she's working these days? can catch her there?"

"I don't. I'm sorry." She gave another shrug moved in a few months ago. We haven't reall know anyone yet."

Alex was typically pretty good at reading thought the woman was telling the truth. He over his shoulder. He motioned to the man his kids. "Any idea if he knew Ruth?"

Even as he asked the question, his atter A rusted-out beige sedan looped around t

Alex continued to scan the area, watching for any sign of trouble.

As they finally headed out of town again, he started to relax.

"I hope that wasn't one of Xavier's men," Claire said. "If it was, that means he's been keeping an eye on Ruth."

"I think if that was one of Xavier's men, we'd know by now. They wouldn't have backed off," Alex said. "Not when they're trying so hard to find you."

Claire's fingers strummed against the steering wheel. "I assume you didn't get anywhere with the neighbor."

"She just moved in. She didn't know Ruth but said a moving van came a few weeks ago." Alex continued to scan his surroundings. He hadn't seen the beige car since leaving the housing development behind. He doubted it would make a reappearance, but that didn't mean he could let his guard down.

"It bothers me that she's no longer at A & M," Claire admitted. "Now her house is for sale. I hope nothing has happened to her."

"I think you need to try A & M again," Alex said.

"Giving out personal information is against company policy."

"I happen to know you can be very persuasive." He gave her a pointed look. "I have a hunch that with a bit of effort, you can get the information you need."

"I'll certainly try. I'm not sure where else to go from here." She ground out a frustrated sigh. "When I left Mia with Beth, I didn't think I'd be gone this long. If I'd known, I'm not sure I would've been able to leave her. I was hoping to buy myself some time, a few days, to find something concrete. It's been weeks and I've hit nothing but dead ends."

He couldn't help but wonder how Mia felt about the

situation, about not seeing her mother for so long. He wondered if she was afraid, lonely, or if Beth was managing to keep her happy.

"I'd like to get into your house," he said, forcing himself to concentrate on the situation at hand. "I want to look through Jared's office myself. See if there's anything you missed. But I'd imagine you have a security system." Claire nodded. "And the police will be keeping an eye on that."

"The police scoured his office when they took his computer. They didn't find anything," Claire said. "At least not that I'm aware of."

"I'd still like to take a look for myself. We should check out of the campground soon," Alex decided. "We can't get another vehicle until we do. It would draw suspicion."

That, of course, was the last thing they wanted.

Before returning to the campground they stopped for much-needed supplies. Alex had grudgingly left Claire in the parking lot. They'd stopped at a convenience store, where he'd made quick time of purchasing a few meals' worth of food. Then—faster than Claire would've believed possible—Alex ran into a department store to buy enough clothing to get him by for a few days. He'd grabbed a duffel bag to stuff everything into and had completed his shopping in record time.

After a quick dinner of canned soup and sandwiches, Claire and Alex sat at the kitchen table to once more look over the names she'd compiled. She'd written down detailed notes about each person. They lived all over the country, with careers in various fields. The one thing they all seemed to have in common was they had money to spend.

Not one of them, as far as Claire's research had found, had a criminal history.

She had to wonder if perhaps they were unaware of the unscrupulous nature of their purchases.

"I spoke with a friend who might be able to dig up some dirt on Xavier," Alex said. "If he's dealing in fenced antiquities, chances are good he's dirtied his hands in other ways, as well."

Claire shook her head. "I've spent hours searching online. I haven't found anything."

Alex flashed a knowing smile. "I'm pretty sure you don't know where to look. Neither do I, for that matter. This friend of mine is a bit of an expert at digging up dirt on people. He has another case that's a priority right now but promised to look into Xavier as soon as he could."

"Would this happen to be a colleague?"

"Yes. I contacted him when I took Roscoe out before dinner," Alex admitted. "He's good with computers. Real good. He can get into databases you or I could never get access to."

"He's a hacker?" Claire asked with arched eyebrows.

"Yes, but he only uses his skills to help people." He leaned back in his seat. "Speaking of hacking, I checked in with Gretchen. The good news is she didn't find any bugs in Beth's house. That means no one has gotten in."

Claire frowned. "How did they track me to the shack?"

"I was getting to that," Alex said. "Gretchen noticed that when Beth takes phone calls, she heads to her office. She has a laptop set up in there. Gretchen suspects—and I think she's probably right—that someone hacked into Beth's webcam. They could get access to Beth's office that way without ever entering her home. They'd only be able to hear her side of the conversation, but in this case, it was all they needed."

Claire nodded thoughtfully. "That makes me feel a bit better. I was worried that if they got into her house once without Beth knowing, that they could do it again."

"I really don't think that's the case," Alex assured her. "I think they accessed our conversation remotely. Needless to say, Gretchen has unplugged the computer and warned Beth and Steven both. I know you hate being away from Mia but being with Beth is probably the safest place for her right now. You couldn't have taken her on the run with you. You would've been too conspicuous. And I don't even want to think about how differently the attack on the shack would've gone if Mia had been inside."

Claire put her hand over her stomach. The very thought made her ill. She couldn't even contemplate how she could've fought off the two men with Mia in tow. She was anxious to move the conversation along.

"Can you tell me what you're doing these days or is it still all very hush-hush?" There was no sarcasm, just curiosity, in her tone.

"I can't tell you everything," he said carefully, "but I can give you an idea of what I do."

She waited for him to go on, surprised that he was willing to reveal anything at all.

"I work for a private organization called HOPE. It's mostly funded by a private benefactor but there are some charities involved." His tone grew serious. "We rescue victims of human trafficking. Or at least, we try to. Most people in this country are blissfully unaware of what an epidemic this has become."

"That sounds dangerous." It also sounded exactly like the sort of organization Alex would be involved in.

"It is. My work takes me all over. I've extracted women from Europe, South America, across the United States.

Not only big cities, but we've broken up a few trafficking rings in small towns you'd never expect."

Claire's stomach clenched. It was horrifying to realize something so awful was taking place in her very own country. Yet she wasn't at all surprised that Alex was a part of trying to set it all right.

"How did you get involved?"

"An army buddy contacted me a few years ago, wondering if I'd be interested in helping out. There was no way I could refuse. The more I learned about HOPE, the more convinced I became that it's where I belong. The woman who founded it nearly lost a daughter to trafficking. She'd gotten tangled up in drugs and became a runaway," he explained. "Her mother, Helena, had the resources to go to great lengths to get her back. Helena realized not everyone did, so she founded HOPE to offer help to others searching for their loved ones."

"It sounds like amazing work." Challenging and heartbreaking yet rewarding. It was exactly the sort of occupation that Claire was sure Alex would thrive in. He could put his military training to use while continuing to make a difference in the world.

"It is. Half the battle is tracking these missing persons down. We have a team specialized in research." He paused. "Mason Berg is part of that team. He's the one that I asked to look into Xavier."

"I'm grateful he's willing to take the time out to help me. Hopefully I'll be able to pay him back someday."

"Don't worry about it. Helping people, that's what the organization is all about. Until I hear back from him, we need to try to figure this out on our own."

"I've told you everything I know."

"Not everything," Alex said gently. "I understand it's

not easy to talk about, but could you walk me through the night Jared died? Maybe there's a clue you missed."

"I've walked myself through it hundreds of times already," Claire admitted. "I can't think of anything out of the ordinary."

"Why was he down by the pool so late at night?" Alex pressed. "Is it possible that he was meeting someone?"

"If he was, I wasn't aware of it. He went down most nights if the weather was nice. It was his evening ritual," she said with a frown. "The first few weeks of our marriage I tried to join him, just to keep him company. He made it clear to me that I wasn't welcome. Some nights he sat in the hot tub, listening to classical music. Other nights he sat poolside, making phone calls. Regardless of how he spent his time, he preferred to do it alone."

She didn't want to know what Alex thought of her pitiful excuse for a marriage. Looking back, she had no doubt Jared had married her because he'd thought it would help him with his business dealings. It was for that same reason he hadn't wanted to let her go. He'd believed it would look bad to the investors of his family-friendly hotel chain if his wife filed for divorce. She realized now that he'd never loved her, and it was not something she cared to talk about.

A quick glance at Alex reassured Claire that he wasn't judging her, that he truly wanted to understand in an effort to be better equipped to help her. She reminded herself that this wasn't personal for Alex. He'd made a career of helping people.

Despite the way her heart fluttered every now and again when she glanced his way, she needed to remember that he was there because she was in a bind. He was there to help her, just like he'd helped dozens of clients. Nothing more, nothing less.

"The night he died," she continued, "was like any other night. He went out to sit on the patio. I read Mia several stories before tucking her in. It wasn't unusual for him to be out rather late. I spent some time reading my Bible."

"You didn't hear anything? See anything?"

"No." She was becoming exasperated. She understood the line of questioning, but just because he continued to ask didn't mean something was going to miraculously come to mind.

"What about Roscoe? Nothing upset him?"

"No. Jared hated having a dog. Roscoe wasn't too fond of him, either. Like most other nights, he was sleeping outside of Mia's bedroom door." She shrugged. "I'm telling you, there was nothing out of the ordinary that night."

"Did you typically go down to check on him?"

Claire closed her eyes, bracing herself against the image his question conjured.

"No," she said, opening them again. She leaned back in her chair and avoided Alex's gaze from across the table. "Our bedroom window overlooked the backyard. I was pulling the curtains closed. I saw him—" she cleared her throat "—saw him floating in the water. He was fully clothed. There really was no question that something was terribly wrong. I raced outside. I didn't even think—I just dove in after him. I was wearing a robe and slippers. The robe dragged me to the bottom. I struggled, finally managing to get it off."

Her head had broken the surface of the water. She'd screamed for help, cried out for someone to assist her as she'd fumbled with her husband's lifeless body, trying to drag him to the edge. She'd managed to climb out and, with strength fueled by adrenaline, she'd managed to tug him onto the pebbly surface surrounding the area. Rescue breathing and CPR had done nothing for Jared, he'd been too far gone.

She pressed her fingers to her lips. They felt cold to her touch as she was slammed with the memory of pressing air into her husband's unresponsive lungs.

There had been so much force behind her chest compressions that she'd cracked his ribs. A sure sign she'd done them correctly.

She'd done everything right, everything within her power to save him.

She'd failed.

And now she was being accused of bringing about his death.

She finally glanced at Alex and was comforted by his sympathetic gaze.

"I know that was an awful thing to experience," he said quietly.

"It was. I tried to save him. I really did."

He took her hand and squeezed. The familiar feel of his fingers around hers brought her comfort. Warmth spilled through her. A subtle echo of past feelings drifted to the surface and she knew she needed to squelch them. She gave Alex's hand a thankful squeeze in return before gently sliding her fingers away. He frowned, probably feeling shunned, but she couldn't worry about that now. Clasping her hands together, she nestled them in the security of her lap.

"I don't doubt that you did everything you possibly could," he said.

"Then you are one of the rare few. It's so disheartening to know that I did all that I could, yet the blame for his death landed on me."

"The case against you primarily stems from the motive of a troubled marriage?" Alex asked.

She hesitated, not because she had anything to hide, but because she hated that there was more.

"Not entirely," she admitted. "That aspect plays a big part, but really it just plays into the larger motive. Jared had me sign a prenup. In the event of a divorce, I got nothing. In the event of his death…"

"His entire estate would go to you," Alex guessed.

"Yes." She shrugged. "He really had no other family. He was an only child, his mother walked out when he was a teenager and his father passed away a few years before we met."

"Considering that you wanted out of the marriage, and he wouldn't let you, to someone who doesn't know you—"

"It could look like I had reason," she finished for him. "His death not only released me from the marriage—"

"But it left you millions."

"It looks bad for me, doesn't it?" Claire asked, though she knew the answer.

"On the flip side, Xavier would've known all of this," Alex said, ignoring her question. "To me that gives him motive for setting you up. He knew you'd be an easy scapegoat."

"I don't think the investigators see it that way."

"We'll have to change that then, won't we?"

"I feel like I'm running out of time," Claire admitted. "I feel like Xavier is closing in on me. I know he wants to get to me before the police do. He wants to silence me."

"He knows you're onto him," Alex agreed. "I think we need to send a copy of these files to the detective working your case." He tapped the black binder. "It can't hurt at this point. If anything, it might detain Xavier for a while."

"I'll do whatever you think is best."

"We won't stay here longer than another night or two,"

Alex continued. "I know of a few campgrounds on public land where you can camp for free. That means no ID required. You just pick a spot and pitch tents."

Claire didn't like that idea at all. It had nothing to do with roughing it and everything to do with the lack of protection a tent offered.

"There are other options," Alex said when he noted her grimace. "Mason—"

"The computer guy?" Claire asked.

"That's him," Alex agreed. "He's been working from home these past few weeks. I know he'd put us up for a few nights. But considering how delicate this situation is, I don't want to involve him unless we're out of options."

"I assume you didn't tell him about me."

"Not directly, but I told him I was in a potentially sticky situation. He agreed to be on standby should we need help." He gave her an apologetic shrug. "He knows I'm traveling with someone. He also knows I need information on Xavier Ambrose. He didn't ask why, but that doesn't mean he hasn't pieced it together himself."

"I'd rather not involve anyone else." Claire didn't want to put anyone else in danger. Nor did she want anyone aware of her situation. Harboring a fugitive could cause all sorts of problems for those involved.

"I don't plan on contacting him again unless it's necessary." Alex strummed a hand against the table. "But I believe strongly in backup plans."

# FIVE

Alex leaned against the door frame, giving Claire her space as she set their plan into motion. Time was running out, their resources were limited, their options were few. This plan had to work.

"Oh, dear, I'm sorry to hear that she left. She worked for A & M for such a long time." Claire paused before pushing ahead with her flawless Southern drawl. "Perhaps you can help me. Ruth is an old friend of mine but the number I have for her has been disconnected." Distress spilled into her tone. She closed her eyes, probably said a silent prayer and went for the information they needed. "I'm planning to be in Portland for the day. I'm not sure when I'll be back. It would be such a *shame* if we weren't able to connect. Could you be a darling and tell me where I could find her?"

Alex waited, sending up a prayer of his own. His teeth clenched when her shoulders drooped. They needed this lead. If it fell through, he wasn't sure where to go from here. Claire's future looked pretty bleak without it. He couldn't bear the thought of that. It made his heart ache to think of Claire behind bars.

Spending time with her the past few days had rekindled a flame that had never really died. He'd left Claire because he'd loved her and he'd thought it was best for her at the time. Over the years he'd managed to dim his feelings. Now he could feel them slowly sparking to life.

He thought he could probably fall back in love if he let himself.

Given Claire's reticence in regard to him, he knew that would be a very bad idea. No, it was better to keep those feelings tamped down. He needed to concentrate on the situation at hand. Spend a little less time contemplating whether or not her skin was still smooth as velvet. His fingers itched to brush against her cheek as a lock of hair escaped from where it had been tucked behind her ear.

"Of course. I understand." Claire sighed. "Unfortunately, I don't know when I'll have the chance to meet up with her again. You see, Ruth's husband passed away several years ago. I'm recently widowed." Her voice crackled with emotion that Alex did not think was fake. "After my husband's death, Ruth sent me the sweetest card and I'd really like to thank her for her kind words. I've been struggling lately. Ruth and her encouragement were such a blessing." She sniffled. "I had really hoped to reconnect with her." There was a pause and then her tone brightened ever so slightly. "Oh, thank you. Of course, I'll keep it to myself."

She twisted around and shot him a hopeful look. He could feel her tension from across the room. He waited impatiently for the call to end.

"You have no idea how much I appreciate it. God bless, have a wonderful day!" She disconnected and held the phone up triumphantly. Her eyes were bright with relief.

"Great job," Alex said. "I take it you received the information we need?"

Claire nodded. "I apologize for the theatrics. I couldn't bring myself to lie, so I had to embellish the truth a bit."

"You got the job done," Alex pointed out. "That's the important thing."

He wasn't sure she'd embellished all that much. Though things had not been good with her husband, she'd still been married to the man. Had lived with him and loved him at one point in time. Of course his death had affected her.

Claire handed his phone to him.

"She's working at a lawyer's office in downtown Portland."

Alex arched an eyebrow. "Interesting career change."

Claire shrugged. "Maybe she feels safer there."

"Did you get an address?"

"I know where this place is. What do you think of heading into the city today?"

Less than two hours later they'd made the trek inland. Alex stood on the sidewalk in front of the Marshall & Clayton Law Firm. He glanced around, as if truly confused about his whereabouts. In gym shorts and a ball cap that he'd confiscated from the campground's lost-and-found box, he looked like any other jogger. He wore sunglasses and earbuds, hoping it would deter anyone from trying to start up a conversation with him. If nothing else, it gave him an excuse to ignore someone if he was spoken to.

His gaze swept the street as he held up a piece of paper. To passersby, it would look as if he were searching for something. In reality, it gave him an excuse to assess potential problems. Nothing seemed amiss. No one appeared suspicious. He didn't think he'd been followed.

Claire was in the Jeep down the block. He hated leaving her unprotected, but having her enter the building with him wasn't an option.

As soon as he decided it was safe, he walked up the sidewalk and pushed through the doors.

He recognized Ruth from the description Claire had given him. Her graying hair was twisted into a tidy bun. She wore silver wire-rimmed glasses. She was a bit on the plain side, but a kind smile swayed her features into pretty.

If he'd had any doubts about her identity, the placard announcing her name would've set him straight.

Alex's gaze darted around the reception area. They were alone. He had no reason to believe Ruth was being watched inside her place of employment. She'd worked for A & M for a long time and she'd know if the lawyer's office had any affiliation with Xavier Ambrose or Jared Mitchell.

"Good afternoon. May I help you?" She studied him, giving him her full attention.

"Actually, I'm hoping you can help a friend of mine." He edged closer to her desk and lowered his voice. "Claire Mitchell?"

"You know Claire? How is she? Is she safe?" The woman's brow furrowed in what Alex would guess was real concern.

"For now," he said. "I was told you recently tried to get in touch with her."

Ruth gave him a pensive look.

"I'm wondering if you're still willing to speak with her." He pulled a burner phone out of his pocket. "If you're willing, Claire can call this number tonight."

"How do I know you're really her friend?" Ruth demanded.

"I guess you'll have to trust me. If you take the phone—" he tried handing it to her but she leaned back in her seat, as if it were contaminated "—she'll call you and you can ask her then."

"I don't think so," Ruth said. "What I have to discuss with Claire, I want to discuss in person. I want to be sure it's her that I'm talking to. It's been a while since we last spoke and even before that, we weren't exactly close, though I do like her. I don't know that I'd recognize her voice. Anyone could pretend to be her."

Alex clenched his jaw, unsure of how to proceed now that the conversation had taken an unexpected turn.

Ruth gave her head a quick, decisive shake. "I don't know you. What I have to say, it could get me in hot water if it got back to the wrong people. I'm not going to take that chance."

"If we agree to meet with you, how can we trust that you won't alert the cops to the meeting?" Alex asked.

A look of indignation instantly flashed across Ruth's face. His intuition told him to take her reaction at face value.

She scowled at him. "Claire Mitchell is innocent! That's the reason I want to talk to her! Why would I ever call the police on her?"

He glanced around, half expecting her angry outburst to draw people out of their offices. When no one came, he tried one more time.

"Please, take the phone. It's safer for Claire that way."

"That might be, but it's safer for me if I know exactly who I'm speaking with," Ruth said stubbornly. "Do you have any idea how many reporters I've had to fend off? I even had to disconnect my phone. I was Jared's secretary for nearly a decade. I suppose they figure I have lots of information on his personal life. And maybe I do. But they realized I'm not willing to share, and they finally went away. When I was at A & M, they were swarming the parking lot. Haven't had one bombard me since I started working here. But how do I know you're not one of them? Claire's disappearance is big news. New information would make headlines. I don't want my words to end up on the front page of tomorrow's paper. What I have to say could get me in a whole heap of trouble with the wrong people."

"I'm not a reporter," Alex insisted.

"I'm not taking the chance that you're fibbing," Ruth replied. She grabbed a pen and turned back to her work, silently dismissing him.

Alex twisted around, was halfway to the door, thinking there was no way Claire could take such a risk. But then a realization crashed in. If Ruth was only willing to speak in person, how could they afford *not* to take that risk?

Claire's disguise was a good one. The public was warned to be on the lookout for a woman and a dog. No one expected her to be with *him*. In a way, being by her side would make her *less* noticeable.

He spun around and stomped back to her desk. "Fine. I'm sure Claire would like to meet as soon as possible."

"I can meet you at the city park tonight," Ruth said. "I don't know you, and I don't have any reason to trust you. I want a setting that's nice and public. How does seven sound?"

It didn't sound good at all, if she wanted the honest truth. He didn't like this plan, but she'd made it clear things were going to be done her way.

"That'll work," he said. "Your willingness to help is greatly appreciated." He pivoted and left the building before Ruth could respond. He scanned the street before he jogged back to the Jeep.

"Was she there?" Claire asked as he slid in.

"She was." He blew out an aggravated sigh. "Only the conversation didn't go anything like I'd hoped."

"I'm not convinced this is a good idea," Alex warned. His fingers were clenched tightly around Claire's. She was aware of his free hand dangling at his side, inches away from the Glock tucked beneath his windbreaker.

"It's the best idea we have," she argued.

They were strolling through the park. Alex had changed out of his running clothes. They were both dressed casually, as if they were nothing more than a young couple in love, out enjoying the beautiful evening.

Even with the constant threat upon them, it was all too easy for Claire to envision just that. Alex's hand around hers felt warm and familiar. It felt comforting. It felt as though it belonged there.

It was hard to imagine that the hand that held hers so reassuringly could also be used to inflict damage when threatened. She knew that during his time in the Rangers, and probably to this day, his body was a finely tuned weapon.

Alex strode with confidence through the park. She knew it wasn't a faked assurance. He faced danger such as this on a regular basis. With that thought, her heart crumpled just a bit. It was a reminder that she was little more than another mission. One he'd assigned to himself, but just another mission nonetheless. She needed to stop thinking about how nice his hand felt, how enticing his woodsy scent was or how the nearness of his body stirred old memories. No good would come from letting her emotions run away with her common sense. Alex would take off as soon as this ordeal was over. And though he may pop into her life when he visited Mia, she needed to remember that it was their daughter who held his interest, not her.

The days of them being a happy couple were in the past and she needed to leave them there.

They had met at a coffee shop while they'd both lived in California, bonding over the fact that they'd both grown up in the Portland area. Claire had been attending college, working on a degree in marketing. Alex had been stationed at a nearby base. They'd dated, fallen in love. He'd proposed before his last deployment. Having finished with school, Claire had returned to Oregon to be near Beth while Alex was away. When his time in the military was completed, he'd joined her.

He hadn't been Stateside long before Claire noticed the change in him. It was a change that seemed to worsen instead of getting better. His last tour had damaged something within him, damaged his soul. She'd known he was hurting and had felt so helpless. It had been a rough time for both of them. They were supposed to be planning a wedding. Alex had refused to pick a date, putting her off each time she'd asked. That's when she'd known their relationship was in serious trouble.

Despite those rocky months, the happy memories by far outnumbered the bad, but it was the bad memories that seemed to carry the most weight. They were heavy, suffocating, with the capacity to drown out everything that was good.

Not that it mattered, she reminded herself. Alex wasn't here to win her back. He was here out of a sense of duty. Though he wouldn't come right out and say it, she knew he felt a sense of obligation.

Yes, he had expressed an intense interest in Mia. For that she was grateful. His interest went no further.

Neither should hers.

She scanned the park, forcing herself to concentrate on the reason they were there.

It was crowded this time of day, with the weather being just right for family outings. Kids ran around playing. Couples were spread out on blankets, picnicking. People were jogging the trails.

"I see her." Her tone held a mixture of excitement and relief. "She's over by the duck pond."

"Let's see what she knows." Alex led the way, her hand still firmly gripped in his.

She knew that behind his dark glasses, he was constantly assessing.

Ruth sat straight, stiff as a statue. She looked nervous as she clutched her purse on her lap.

Alex and Claire casually walked up to the bench.

Ruth glanced at them, looked away, then swiveled her head as her gaze zeroed in first on Alex and then on Claire.

She got to her feet and pulled Claire into a hug.

"I didn't recognize you at first. I've been so worried about you!" she exclaimed. "When they said you ran off, I was afraid it was a lie. I was afraid you'd met the same fate as your husband." Ruth gave Claire a final squeeze before releasing her.

She eyed up Alex warily.

Claire was concerned about how scandalous this might look to Ruth. Her husband had only been gone for a little over a month. Here she was, approaching with another man.

Alex must've come to the same conclusion. "Claire and I are friends from way back," he said, "her college days actually. When I heard about the ludicrous accusation against her, I knew I had to do whatever I could to help."

"Friends?" Ruth asked as she settled back onto the bench. "That's unfortunate. Claire's a good woman. She deserves to have a good man in her life. I'd say if you're willing to help her out of this mess that would make you qualified for the job."

Alex chuckled.

Claire blushed as she took a seat next to Ruth.

"It's such a lovely evening!" She glanced around, looking for any sign of trouble. Really, she knew she didn't have to bother. Alex already had it covered. "It looks as if the ducks are enjoying themselves."

A pair of young children stood on the small pier that protruded into the lake. They tossed bread crumbs to the energetic ducks.

"Changing the topic doesn't change the facts," Ruth said. "Now let's get down to why we're here."

"Your phone call," Claire agreed. "You said you had information that might help me. As you can imagine, I'm desperate for any information that could help clear my name." She paused for a heartbeat. "I didn't kill Jared."

"Of course you didn't," Ruth said vehemently. "I don't believe for one second that you had anything to do with Jared's death."

"Thank you."

Alex remained standing, a hip cocked against the bench as he kept watch.

"I shouldn't speak ill of the dead, but my dear Charles never did trust Jared or Xavier," Ruth admitted. "He asked me many times to find a different job over the years. It's ironic that now that Charles and Jared are both gone, I've done just that."

"I wish you could've left under better circumstances," Claire said.

"That's nothing for you to worry about," Ruth assured her. "I'm happy you tracked me down. I couldn't continue to work at A & M, not when I was forced to listen to the way Xavier spoke about you."

"What has Xavier been saying about me?"

"That Xavier, his lips have been flapping nonstop since Jared died. I'm not one for gossip. If you and your husband were having marital problems that should've been between the two of you," she said with a frown. "It's not his place to be spouting off about it."

Claire and Alex shared a look. Neither was surprised by this revelation. Of course Xavier would be doing what he could to perpetuate the rumor that Claire and Jared had a rocky marriage.

"He said you complained of how many hours Jared had to work. That you were always nagging him about being gone so much."

"That's not true." If anything, she was grateful for the time he was away. The house was more peaceful with him gone. It was hardly as if she could admit that, though.

"What else did he say?" Alex asked.

Ruth frowned at him.

"I'm not asking for gossip," he clarified. "The fact is, it could help Claire to know what rumors she's up against."

"He said that Jared had been talking about divorcing you."

Claire frowned. She doubted that very much. When she'd suggested it, she'd ended up paying for it dearly.

"According to him, because you signed one of those prenuptial agreements, you wouldn't get a penny. To hear him tell it, you killed Jared so you wouldn't lose out on his millions."

Claire sighed and shook her head. "I've never cared about the money."

Ruth placed her hand over Claire's. "I believe you. You never seemed the type. I also know you'd never leave the country and leave that darling girl of yours behind, like he's claiming."

"I wouldn't," she agreed. Xavier wanted to find her first. She thought he was pushing that story, hoping the police would waste their resources searching elsewhere.

"He said you've got quite the temper," Ruth continued. "He said Jared confided in him frequently about it. I don't believe that, either. Anyone who would believe such a thing would be a fool."

"Unfortunately," Claire said, "not everyone is as levelheaded as you. I'm sure there are plenty of people at the office who are going to buy into what he's saying."

A nagging suspicion told her he'd repeated this story to the police, as well. If they took him at his word, her motives for killing her husband were stacking up.

"That's why I wanted to pass along a conversation I heard."

Claire glanced at Alex again.

"Go on," he gently encouraged Ruth.

"I was in the building a bit later than usual one night," Ruth began. "I had been in the basement looking through the storage room for an old paper file. When I came upstairs, the two of them were going at it something fierce. Xavier accused Jared of stealing something from him. Something important. Jared didn't deny it. I heard Xavier tell Jared that if he didn't return what was his, he wouldn't live to regret it."

"Sounds awfully close to a death threat, if you ask me," Alex said.

Ruth nodded. "That's what I thought."

"Why didn't you tell the police?" Alex asked.

Ruth dropped her gaze and began to fidget with the straps of her purse. "I should have. I just couldn't. I was afraid. There was something in his tone I'd never heard before, a fierceness laced with so much hatred. It rattled me." She turned to Claire, the fear evident in her eyes.

The woman was still afraid and it made her even more grateful that she had showed up.

"I understand," Claire said softly. "Xavier is a powerful man."

"The tension in the office the last few months had been almost unbearable. Xavier was traveling more than usual. I was happy about that," Ruth confided. "There was less arguing because he was gone."

Alex gave Claire a look that she easily read. Xavier had conveniently been out of town the night Jared had been killed. Had he beefed up his travel schedule recently so as not to raise suspicion about being away?

"I wish I had more to tell you. But that's really all I know." She paused. "Actually, there is one other thing. I'm not sure if it's relevant because it didn't make much sense to me."

They both looked at her expectantly.

"Your husband told Xavier that he had an insurance policy protecting against his termination."

Claire swiveled her head to look at Alex once more. His jaw was clenched.

"His termination?" Claire asked as she returned her attention to Ruth.

Ruth's eyebrows scrunched in confusion. "I was always under the impression they were partners. I didn't realize Xavier could fire him. But it's not as if I'd be privy to that information. Regardless, your husband said that he knew Xavier had a history of terminating people. He said the policy was in your possession."

"Excuse me?" Claire blurted.

"Xavier was furious," Ruth admitted. "He said your husband didn't have the right to share the details of the business with you. Jared assured him he hadn't, that you would only open the policy if necessary."

"Did he say anything else?" Claire pressed. This was the first she'd heard mention of any sort of policy. She had scoured Jared's office. She had run across no such thing.

Ruth's eyebrows puckered as if straining to remember. "He told Xavier that if he were terminated, this policy could take down the entire operation. He laughed—your husband did. He said that if Xavier tried to take him down, they'd go down together."

Claire's gaze locked with Alex's. Jared had been foolish to provoke Xavier. He had done worse than provoke him, he had practically dared him.

"Claire," Ruth said, dropping her tone, "I hope you don't think badly of me for saying this, but I've begun to suspect that your husband and Xavier may have been partaking in illegal activities."

She nodded somberly. "I believe you may be right."

"I worked for A & M for years. I knew both Jared and Xavier were ruthless businessmen, but I never had reason to think they were dangerous." Ruth glanced over her shoulder, as if afraid her old employers were standing behind her. "Xavier changed the last few months. After I overheard the argument, I didn't feel comfortable around him. I started noticing little things. He seemed angry all the time. More and more, he'd keep his office door shut. I think he must've been on the phone quite a bit because I could hear him talking, but he was always alone. After the evening of their argument, it seemed he went out of the way to be friendly with your husband, but it seemed forced. Or perhaps my perception was warped."

Claire doubted that. She had to assume Xavier had been striving to keep up appearances.

"I understand that it would be difficult," Alex said, "but I wish you would reconsider going to the police with this information. It really could help Claire."

Ruth lifted a trembling hand to her mouth. "I've suspected Xavier played a part in Jared's death. I'm right, aren't I?"

"Yes." Alex's answer was blunt.

"We think so, too," Claire agreed.

Ruth nodded as she gazed across the pond. "The thought has crossed my mind, but I wanted to be wrong. If it's true, then Xavier is a very dangerous man. Jared's death has troubled me from the start. It's the reason I moved into a secure apartment building. If I went to the police—" she shook her head helplessly "—and he found out, there could be trouble for me. I have grandkids who stay with me on the weekends. I can't risk having him come after me, or worse, my family."

"I understand," Claire said. "I'm grateful that you met with us today. Your information might prove to be invaluable."

"You were always so kind to me. You always took the time to chat. Not like that unfriendly woman Xavier is married to," Ruth said. "I've been keeping you in my prayers." She twisted her fingers around Claire's hand once more. "I'll continue to pray for you until justice is served."


"I'm not positive," Alex said as he studied the rearview mirror, "but I think we're being followed."

He veered to the right, without the courtesy of a blinker, and took the exit. The vehicle followed. As it angled onto the exit, Claire got a good look at it.

"It's a dark sedan, either black or navy blue. There are at least two people in it." She glanced at Alex. "How long have they been following us?"

"I spotted them a few blocks from the park. But there were a lot of people coming and going," he said. "It wasn't until this last turnoff that I knew for sure. I'd guess Xavier has had someone following Ruth. Maybe he knew about her phone call. Or maybe she was acting guilty before she resigned. They probably followed her to the park and have been biding their time."

They'd known from the start that meeting with Ruth was a huge risk. But with her being the only potential lead, and with her being so stubborn, it was a risk they'd been forced to take. The information she'd shared could prove to be priceless.

If only they had the opportunity to pursue what they'd learned.

It seemed Xavier's resources were endless.

Claire released a growl of frustration. "They couldn't go after us in the park. There were too many people. And—"

"And it wouldn't fit into the scenario Xavier has built around you being the murderer if someone took you out in such a public place," Alex said, finishing her thought. "It would look too suspicious."

Claire winced. If Xavier got to her, if he killed her, he would make sure there were no witnesses.

"We're certainly not in a public place now." Claire eyed the empty road ahead with trepidation.

"Here they come," Alex said under his breath. He reached for his Glock. He drove with his left hand while holding the gun in the right. "Hold on tight," he said to Claire. "We're going for a ride."

Claire gripped the dash when she realized what Alex was about to do. A fenced-in cow pasture was to their left. A harvested field to their right. He whipped the Jeep to the right. As he did, a bullet tore through the back side window. If he'd continued straight, the bullet likely would've hit him or Claire.

Claire took the gun from Alex's hand as he drove down the ditch and up into the harvested field. When Alex pivoted the Jeep around so they were headed in the opposite direction, Claire propped her elbows in the window frame and fired off several shots. At least one bullet hit its target. A tire exploded, sending the car fishtailing wildly. It careened into the ditch, where it skidded up the side and into the field.

Retaliation shots were fired, but they missed their mark.

Without slowing, Alex maneuvered the Jeep onto the road and sped back toward the highway. Claire twisted around to check out the car. It wobbled back and forth, as if the driver was trying to reverse it but the vehicle wouldn't cooperate.

"You're a great shot," Alex said, his voice rising in surprise.

"Of course I am," Claire replied, her body now buzzing with adrenaline. "I had a great teacher."

When they'd been together, Alex had never liked that Claire lived alone. Early in their relationship he'd insisted she get a handgun.

And learn to shoot it.

They'd spent countless hours at the local shooting range.

Alex glanced over his shoulder to assess the damage in the back seat. "We'll have to take the top off before we go back to the campground."

The bullet had gone in through the back passenger-side window and exited out the other side.

Claire dropped down in her seat. Her adrenaline rush evaporating as reality sank in.

The thick plastic that comprised the windows of the

soft-top Jeep cover flapped in the wind. Gaping holes existed where the windows should've been.

"They could've killed us," Claire said, her voice tight with emotion.

"Yeah," Alex said with a hard edge to his tone. "I'm pretty sure that was the plan."

# SIX

They had driven around at length the night before to be sure they weren't followed by another car. Eventually, Alex pulled over on a deserted road to remove the damaged canvas top. He'd stuffed it under the back seat so as not to raise suspicion at the campground.

Claire thought they might raise suspicion regardless. She'd been relieved when they'd reached the cabin, where Roscoe had enthusiastically greeted them.

In the morning, dark clouds threatened rain. It made no sense to take the top off today, of all days.

Claire had called Ruth to check on her. She was grateful to hear the woman had made it home safely, probably in large part thanks to crowded streets and her secure parking garage. She warned her that she might be in danger. Her friend had taken the news with a calmness she hadn't expected. Ruth promised that—despite being new at her job—she would take some time off, sequestering herself in the safety of her apartment. Though her new employer might not be happy about the request, Ruth's safety was of the utmost importance.

She knew their lives had been spared by God's grace. It gave her hope that He wasn't done with her yet and that He would lead her out of this tribulation. Despite that hope, she had slept more fitfully than usual that night. Not only was she haunted by her usual nightmares, she now suffered from the nagging thought that she was missing something.

"We need to get back into your house," Alex said as he finished off his coffee.

"I went through his office," Claire reminded him. "I went through his files, one paper at a time. I went through the files on his laptop, through his desk drawers. I even got down on my hands and knees to look under the chairs and to be sure nothing was taped to the bottom of the desk. I looked everywhere I could think of, hoping I would find evidence that Xavier had killed someone prior to Jared. If some sort of insurance policy existed, don't you think I would've run across it?"

"It's doubtful he would've kept it in his business office," Alex said. "It would be too easy for Xavier to find it. It's also doubtful he would've put it in a safe-deposit box. Not if it's something he *wanted* you to run across."

"I've thought of all that, as well," Claire admitted.

Alex set his mug down, looking grim. "There's always the possibility that he was bluffing."

"I know." Claire slowly spun her own mug of coffee around on the table. "It's a possibility, but Jared was a man of action. If the thought crossed his mind that he needed some sort of insurance—"

"He would've put it in place," Alex finished.

Claire nodded.

"If such a policy exists, he wouldn't have hidden it so well it couldn't be found. Otherwise, what would be the point?"

"But he wouldn't have wanted it to be found *too* easily, either."

"Of course," Alex said, "it would sure help if we knew exactly what it was that we were looking for."

Roscoe loped up to Alex and nudged his hand. He grinned at the dog. "Hey, boy, you finally want to be my pal again?"

Claire smiled. She had noticed that Roscoe didn't favor Alex. He came to her when he wanted attention, and if Alex took over, the dog didn't mind. He'd even trot over to Alex when called, but he never sought Alex out, until now.

"I think he's been holding a grudge," Alex accused. "He's pretty mad at me for leaving. Hopefully he's decided to forgive me." He turned his attention to the dog and gave him a good rubdown. Without looking at Claire he said, "I sure hope he's not the only one who's managed to forgive me."

She reached across the table, taking his hand. His eyebrows hoisted ever so slightly in surprise. She squeezed his fingers, wishing things were different. Wishing they'd never lost the closeness they'd once shared. For Mia's sake, and their own, they needed to find peace with the past.

"I forgave you a long time ago." She had forgiven him because that's what she knew God wanted her to do. Forgiveness hadn't come quickly, but over time she had realized that holding on to her anger was pointless.

Alex's eyes met hers. "I appreciate that."

"But that doesn't mean that you walking out on me doesn't still hurt," she admitted. "Just because I've forgiven you, that doesn't mean that I'm okay with what happened."

Alex sighed. "I understand."

Roscoe let out an aggrieved whine.

"He's been cooped up a lot the last few days. I should

run up and down the trail with him, let him get some exercise," Alex suggested as his hand slid from hers.

"He'd like that."

"I won't go far."

Once he was gone Claire went to her bedroom to sort through her belongings. She grabbed the last clean outfit she had along with her toiletry bag. The past few days had been so rushed. She looked forward to luxuriating in a long, hot shower. It felt like it had been years since she'd been afforded such a luxury. The truck stop showers ran on quarters. Though she knew she had plenty of cash, it seemed silly to waste it on water. Her showers had been hurried.

Ten minutes later, smelling like honeysuckles courtesy of the shampoo she had packed, she emerged feeling refreshed.

As she was scrubbing off she heard the front door open. She had timed her shower perfectly. She wondered if Alex would be willing to go to the nearest town for dinner. They could run through a drive-through. She was starving, but more than that, she was starting to feel stir-crazy. Maybe they could find a quiet park to eat at.

She dressed and then wrapped the towel around her head.

"So I was thinking—" she said as she tugged open the door. She immediately cut herself off when she realized she was looking into the eyes of a stranger.

Her hand reflexively flew to her neck, searching for the bottle of pepper spray she wore like a security blanket. Fresh out of the shower, she hadn't put it on yet.

"I'm so sorry! I knocked," the middle-aged woman explained. "I didn't think anyone was here." She held up a bottle of cleaning fluid. "I was going to spruce the place up a bit."

"Oh, you don't have to do that." Claire struggled for calm. "We're fine without housekeeping services."

"But—" The woman—Rhonda, according to her name tag—paused. She narrowed her eyes at Claire.

"We're not very messy," Claire quickly said. "I don't mind straightening up myself."

"Sure." Rhonda reached for the basket that held her cleaning supplies. Her gaze zeroed in on the couch where Alex's pillow and blanket were, again, neatly stacked. Her brow puckered for a moment before she turned to Claire and gave her a strained smile.

Was she simply wondering why one of them was sleeping on the couch? Or did her curiosity run deeper than that?

Dread, slow and nauseating, began to course through Claire's veins. She turned away from Rhonda, trying to act casual as she reached for the coffee cups that had been left on the table. She wanted the woman gone but wanted to be subtle about it. Desperation could ignite the woman's suspicion. She had a feeling it might be too late.

The cabin door swung open. Roscoe trotted in but Alex paused on the threshold. His eyes widened almost imperceptibly when he realized Claire wasn't alone.

"Oh, hey, Renee," he said, intentionally calling her by her middle name, "I didn't realize you had company. It's starting to drizzle out, so we decided to cut our walk short."

Claire forced a casualness she didn't feel. "She was just wondering if we needed any housekeeping services." Her eyes were on Alex. Perhaps she was being paranoid but she felt as if she could feel Rhonda's eyes roving over her.

"I think we're good," Alex said lightly as he strode into the room. "But thanks."

Rhonda hefted her basket onto her hip. "If you're sure. Just stop by the office if you need anything."

"Thank you, we'll do that," Claire said.

The moment the door was closed, Alex spun to face her. "What was that all about?"

Claire shrugged helplessly. "She came in while I was in the bathroom. She said she knocked, but I didn't hear her."

His jaw clenched as he turned to face the door.

"Do you think she recognized me?"

He turned back to study her face. "You're not in much of a disguise. The towel is covering your hair but other than that, you look like you." He strummed his hand on his thigh. "On the other hand, she didn't seem jittery."

"I felt like she was staring at me. Studying me or something."

"Maybe we should head out," Alex suggested. "It's probably time even if she didn't recognize you. Let's pack up. We'll leave within the hour. If we leave right now, it might seem suspicious."

Claire returned to the bathroom, where she quickly brushed out her hair. She hung up the towel before repacking her toiletry bag. When she came out of the bathroom, Alex's duffel bag was packed, sitting by the door.

Roscoe sat off to the side, watching the commotion with curiosity.

Thunder rumbled menacingly in the distance, a promise of the storm to come.

Claire wrapped her arms around her stomach, trying to quench the nausea she felt. "I'm so sorry."

"It's okay. None of this is your fault."

His arms slipped around her waist. She slid hers around his neck as she rested her head against his chest. She wanted to melt into him. She had always felt so safe in Alex's arms. Reminding herself the situation was temporary, she allowed herself a few moments of bliss. His body felt so strong, so capable. His scent reminded her of days long ago.

"I should've been listening. Or I should've waited to shower." Her words were muffled.

He gave her a squeeze and she looked up into his familiar brown eyes. "If you want to play that game, I could say I should've been watching. Quite frankly, I should've been. I just thought it would be good for Roscoe to get a good run in so we went a little farther than we should have."

"I'm so glad you're here," she murmured.

"Me, too."

Her heart fluttered in a way it had no business fluttering. Alex's arms around her felt right. She could tell herself she was over him, but she wasn't. She wasn't sure she would ever be. But he wasn't right for her. She needed a man who could commit. Who could put family before work. Someone who wouldn't run off when things got tough.

"Claire?" Alex's voice was a low rumble, vibrating against her chest as he still held her close.

She realized she'd been gazing at him, lost in her thoughts, wishing things were different. Wishing he'd never left all those years ago. His deep coffee-colored eyes bore into her, as if struggling to read her mind. She became vividly aware of how intently he was studying her.

When he lowered his mouth to hers, she enjoyed the sweetness of his kiss just briefly before coming to her senses. She gently put her hands against his chest, putting some space between them.

"That's not a good idea," she said quietly.

Alex's jaw clenched for a moment before he gave a sharp nod. "Right. Of course. I don't know what I was thinking. I guess I just got caught up in the moment."

Claire tucked a strand of hair behind her ear. "We both did."

Before she could worry about what else to say, Roscoe let out a low growl. He jumped up and scampered to the door, baring his teeth. The grating sound of his unrest filled the room.

Alex immediately moved to the window, his body tense. He slid his phone out of his pocket and tapped something across the screen.

"What's that about?" Claire asked.

He nodded toward the parking lot. "We're about to have company. I figure now is a good time to put that backup plan into motion."

"Care to elaborate?"

"Later. Right now you need to get in the other room," Alex commanded.

Claire knew better than to argue. Had the woman recognized her? Had she come this far only to be caught by one careless act? She grabbed Roscoe and moved to the bedroom, closing the door behind them.

Claire disappeared into her bedroom and seconds later a series of knocks erupted on the other side of the front door. Alex peered out the window, not surprised to see Tom, the owner standing there.

He'd met Tom the night he'd checked in and had seen him puttering around outdoors a few times. He had seemed friendly enough. Alex hoped that if the man was suspicious he could defuse the situation.

"Hi, Tom," he said as he opened the door. "What can I do for you?"

Tom was short, wiry, bald, with a pair of bushy gray eyebrows. They were scrunched together at the moment, as if something disturbed him. He tried to peer over Alex's shoulder. "Oh, just wondering if you're enjoying your stay."

"We are. This is a nice place you have." Alex kept his tone light as he stood in the doorway. "It's quiet, rustic, a great place to relax."

"Is the missus enjoying it all right?"

Alex made a hesitant face. "She would be, if she was feeling better. It's unfortunate timing, but she hasn't been feeling well the last few days," he said, unable to forget for a second how stressed Claire had been. "She's lying down right now."

"I see. I was wondering why I haven't seen her around much."

Alex gave him a conspiratorial grin and lowered his voice. "Between you and me? She's not real outdoorsy. She thinks she is. Likes the *idea* of the outdoors, but when it comes right down to it, she's not real crazy about bugs, dirt, too much sun. She'd rather spend her time indoors reading." He shrugged. "To each their own, right? We were just looking to get away, get some relaxation in. If she'd rather stay inside and read," he said, his thoughts flashing to the black binder Claire had been poring over, "I guess that's all right by me."

"I s'pose some people prefer being indoors," Tom agreed. "Can't say I see the appeal."

Alex wanted to prolong the conversation. "Is there something I can help you with?" he asked.

"I guess if you could tell me how long you plan to stay, that would be a help. You booked through the weekend but said you might check out early. It would be handy to know your plan if we start getting calls."

"I think we'll head out in the morning," Alex said.

"Heading anywhere in particular?"

"I'm not sure what the next few days will bring," Alex admitted. "We don't have any definite plans. Maybe we'll even take a drive down the coast before heading home."

Tom cocked his head to the side. "Where's home?"

"Portland," Alex replied easily enough. He'd put a fake address on the registration form when he'd checked in, but the city was correct.

"Too big of a city for me," Tom replied.

Alex nodded in agreement. "Yeah. That's why it's nice to get away sometimes."

"If your wife is so fond of the indoors, this seems like an odd pick." Tom frowned. "If you'll forgive me for saying so."

Alex had never claimed Claire to be his wife, but if that's the assumption Tom had made, he sure wasn't about to correct him.

"It seemed like a good compromise. She's not finicky. And the price was right." Alex gave a carefree shrug. He hoped the battered Jeep would give credence to his statement. "We were looking for a getaway that wouldn't drain our bank account."

"All right then." Tom took a step away. "I apologize for the intrusion. Enjoy the rest of your day."

"You, too, sir," Alex said with a nod. He didn't mind spending the time talking with Tom. The longer he delayed the man, the more time it gave his buddy Mason.

He closed the door as Tom backed away. He didn't think it was his imagination. There was definitely something off about the conversation. Tom had been digging for information. Alex wasn't sure he'd satisfied the man's curiosity.

He could beat himself up over his error in judgment—

he should've stayed within view of the cabin—but he'd learned long ago there was no point. He couldn't always control every situation. He'd finally accepted that God was in control. And while he could do his best, the outcome would ultimately be up to Him.

*Please God*, he prayed silently, *You've gotten me out of tough spots before. Please get Claire and me out of this one.*

The bedroom door creaked open. Claire stayed on the other side, looking worn and weary. "He suspects, doesn't he?"

"I think so. It didn't seem like Rhonda recognized you," Alex said. "But maybe your face clicked into place after she walked out."

"I knew I felt her studying me. She must've been trying to place me."

Alex wedged himself close to the window, trying to stay hidden behind the curtain. The drizzle had turned into fat drops of rain. It came down sideways, slashing across the pane. He caught sight of Tom talking to Rhonda. They were eyeing up the Jeep as they stood under the eve of the office.

"This doesn't look good," Alex said. He moved away from the window, nudging Claire back toward the bedroom. "Tom just pulled out his phone. We need to move." He was pretty sure he knew who Tom was about to call.

Claire didn't need to be told twice. She pivoted, heading back inside.

Alex grabbed his duffel bag, then dug enough cash out of his wallet to cover their stay. He tossed it on the table. Seconds later, when he reached Claire's bedroom, the only room with a window on the backside of the cabin, she was already pulling off the screen. Alex gave Claire a leg up, helping her through. She landed with a graceful thud on the muddy ground.

She blinked against the deluge but instantly reached up to help assist Roscoe through the opening.

"Come on, boy." Her voice was an octave above a whisper and wouldn't carry far due to the incoming storm. Alex lifted him from inside the cabin. The dog leaped out and looked back at them with excitement.

Alex was out the window in seconds, landing with less grace than either Claire or Roscoe.

They were off and running the moment his feet hit the ground. He took the lead, heading through the woods, looping toward the road. He didn't know these woods well enough to stray too far. What he did know was that they were going to stay away from the trails that ran through the property. He tried to stay close enough to the road leading in to keep his bearings.

The rain made the foliage slick. The fat droplets that continued to fall made it difficult to see. Alex sent a text as they ran. It was impossible to guess how much time they had. If a deputy was in the area, he could arrive in a matter of minutes.

"Alex," Claire intoned, "this is so bad. What are we going to do? Where are we going to go? Without the Jeep, we're not going to make it very far."

He ducked out of the way of a low-slung branch. Roscoe trotted alongside them, not minding the rain in the least.

"I've got it handled." He hoped. "Remember when I told you it's always a good idea to have a backup plan? This is why."

Claire's backpack flopped around, throwing her off balance. She slipped but caught herself before she fell. Already, her hair was slick, stuck to her head like a cap.

Droplets streamed down her face and she fruitlessly wiped them away.

"Are you going to elaborate on this plan?" she asked.

Alex's phone pinged with a text message. He was relieved to see Mason had sent him an estimated time of arrival.

"We need to get to the gas station down the road," Alex said. "My friend will meet us there."

Claire clutched at his arm, slowing him down, but he'd already caught sight of what had her suddenly concerned. She tugged at him, pulling him behind a pine tree. The wide boughs offered coverage.

Flashing lights splashed color through the forest as a cruiser rolled along the gravel drive that led to the campground. The siren was off, meaning the officer didn't want to scare the suspects away.

He had no doubt they were the suspects being sought out.

For the first time Alex was grateful for the rain. It streamed over the windows of the car. The wipers swished, trying to keep up. More than likely the deputy was concentrating on the road ahead. If he looked out the side window, the rain was so heavy he probably wouldn't see much.

"Keep moving," Alex ordered as soon as it was past. He darted out from behind the huge fir and Claire followed. "We need to put as much distance as possible between us and the cabin."

"Then what?" Claire demanded. "As soon as they realize we're gone, they'll spread out the search."

"It might take them a while," Alex said. "In cases like yours, people call in leads all the time. Law enforcement is obligated to check them out. Tom and Rhonda only suspect. It will take the deputy some time to verify."

Unfortunately they'd probably speed the process along. Tom had been in front of the cabin since speaking with Alex. He would know that they hadn't left the cabin through the front door.

Innocent people didn't typically crawl out windows, leaving their vehicle behind.

"We'll be long gone by then." His tone was firm.

"Your colleague?" Claire guessed.

"Yes. Mason prefers to be hands-on working in the field, but he happens to be doing some computer support work from home right now. When I contacted him he told me to let him know if I needed anything." Alex had helped Mason out a few times and Mason was more than willing to reciprocate. "When things started looking dicey just now, I sent him a text asking if he could meet us at the gas station down the road. It's about three miles away."

"Three miles?" Claire panted.

"You used to run daily," Alex said. "Have you kept up with the habit?"

"Until I've been in hiding, yes."

"Even with Mia?"

"They have this wonderful invention called a jogging stroller," she said wryly. "However, I can guarantee I can run faster if I don't waste my breath on talking."

Alex didn't argue.

The weather made for slow going. In no time their clothes were soaked, their shoes saturated. The rain bit at his face and he knew Claire had to be cold. She didn't complain. He set a steady pace and she managed to keep up.

When they reached the main road, they veered in the direction of the gas station while staying hidden in the foliage.

He noted Claire was pressing a hand to her side.

"You okay?" he asked.

She nodded. "Slogging through the mud and jumping over fallen logs is quite the workout. I guess the last few weeks have left me more out of shape than I thought."

Alex didn't waste any more energy on words. They ran parallel to the main road. Every now and again a car whizzed by. They stayed far enough back that they shouldn't be spotted.

Running three miles used to be nothing to Claire, but under the conditions, she seemed to be slowing down.

His phone buzzed and he tugged it from his pocket. He had to ease his pace to read the message. Relief hit him when he read the text. He strained his eyes, looking through the rain and the trees. Up ahead he spotted a vehicle pulled over on the side of the road.

"Looks like we're not going to have to go all the way to the gas station after all," he said.

"Is that him?" Claire asked. "Your friend?"

"Yes."

They pushed themselves the rest of the way.

When they neared, Alex realized Mason had his hood up. If anyone drove by, they'd assume car trouble. It gave him a reason to be pulled over.

As they reached the vehicle Alex scanned the road. A car was heading toward them, so they stayed back. It sped by. A string of three cars crested the hill in the opposite direction. He was simultaneously relieved yet disheartened that not one vehicle stopped to help Mason.

"The coast is clear. Let's go." He gave Claire a push and they bolted out of the woods with Roscoe by their side. He tugged open the back door of the double cab, allowing Claire, then the dog to scramble in. He slid into the front seat, grateful to have made it this far.

Another vehicle appeared in the distance as it rounded the curve ahead.

Mason slammed the hood shut.

He was as drenched as they were when he slid into his driver's seat. Looking over his shoulder, he cast a curious glance at Claire. If she looked familiar, he hid it well.

"Thanks for the ride," she said weakly.

"No problem."

Mason fired up the engine and pulled onto the road. As he did, two cruisers came flying around the curve, lights flashing.

"I'm not even going to ask if those are for you," he said calmly.

Alex gave him a nod as he looked back at Claire. She was slouched down in the seat, shivering as she watched the cruisers speed past.

He cranked up the heat.

"I'm heading out tomorrow," Mason said. "You're welcome to my house if you need a place to stay."

"I was hoping you'd say that," Alex admitted. He was also relieved Mason would be gone. He didn't want to make his friend any more of an accomplice than he already unknowingly was.

"How about a vehicle?" Mason asked.

"It would be greatly appreciated," Alex said.

"You've bailed me out more times than I care to admit." Mason shot him a look. "The least I can do is try to return the favor."

# SEVEN

"I hate to ask," Alex began and Mason slid a glance his way, "but we left in such a hurry. Roscoe is going to need food by the end of the day."

They'd been driving for some time. Claire had constantly checked the back window, sure they were being followed. So far, they seemed to be in the clear.

"No problem," Mason said. "As soon as I find somewhere to stop, I'll run in and grab something."

The rain had faded to a light mist. The truck's wipers intermittently swiped back and forth in a rhythmic motion. They'd be at Mason's soon.

Even though they were safe for the moment, Claire's heart was still pounding. Despite the heat blasting, she was chilled all the way through. Her feet were icy, her shoes soggy. She clenched her jaw to keep her teeth from chattering. She was miserable, but she was relieved that they had gotten away.

It had been a close call. Too close. She hated putting Alex at risk like that.

She knew it wouldn't be long until they determined that she had, indeed, been a guest at A Place in the Pines. Until now, it was suspected that she had crossed into Canada. As soon as they realized she'd been in the area, they were going to intensify their search. She feared her time for going after Xavier had passed.

She felt as though her freedom was slipping away.

She hated the thought of taking Alex down with her. She still cared about him, there was no denying that. Even if a relationship couldn't go anywhere. Her mind spun when she thought of that kiss. Unfortunately, she couldn't help but wonder what Alex's motives were.

Did he feel guilty about walking away from her and from Mia? She knew how Alex handled his guilt. He always struggled to find a way to set things right. Could that have been what the kiss was about? Had he decided to try to revive what they'd once had in an effort to set the past right?

To relieve his guilt?

Claire didn't want to be with him because he felt obligated.

She firmly reminded herself she had no business wanting to be with him at all. She couldn't risk giving him her heart again—if he even wanted it—not when he'd left her so shattered the first time.

"This place looks as good as any," Mason said. He flipped on his blinker and turned into a large gas station on the edge of town. He parked on the side of the building, away from the windows. "Need anything else?"

"I'm good," Claire said.

"Me, too," Alex agreed. He handed Mason some cash and then Claire and Alex were alone.

Alex twisted around in the seat. "How are you doing?"

"Happy to be out of the woods. Literally."

This was the first business they'd seen in miles. The parking lot was fairly full. The rain had completely subsided now, leaving a silvery gray sky behind.

She tried not to think of the chaos most likely taking place at the campground.

"I'm also worried," she continued. "I don't want to get your friend in trouble. He seems like a really nice guy."

"He is."

"I don't like the thought of putting him at risk," Claire admitted.

"I don't, either, but we really don't have a choice. I trust Mason. Working with HOPE, we sometimes have to work outside of the laws of man. Sometimes a rescue depends on it. We don't like it, but sometimes that's just the way it is."

"Do you think he knows who I am?" Claire was sure he knew but was hoping Alex would assure her otherwise.

"I think it's likely." Alex's expression darkened. "Get down. Get down!"

Claire didn't question him. She dropped down in the seat as far as she could go.

Alex casually turned toward the front. Looking out the passenger window, he said, "Don't panic, but a patrol car just pulled up."

Claire didn't have much control over her fright. It hit her hard, stole her breath.

Alex continued speaking while looking away from the driver's side. "She's parked right next to us."

"Did she see me?" Claire's voice trembled. She wasn't sure how much more of this she could take. Constantly living in fear, it was getting to be too much. Maybe she should just surrender. She wasn't guilty. Law enforcement would figure that out, wouldn't they? The only thing she was guilty of was running from a crime she hadn't committed.

Alex casually turned back around. "She's still sitting

in the car. Looks like she's talking to someone, either on the phone or the radio." He leaned forward, took a map out of the glove compartment and busied himself pretending to study it.

"What if someone saw Mason's truck?" Claire asked. "What if someone called in his license plate?"

She had thought the way was clear when they'd raced through the ditch, but what if it hadn't been?

Roscoe was on the floor. His stubby tail thumped slowly as he eyed her up. His head was cocked, as if he understood her concern.

"Don't borrow trouble, Claire."

Alex's tone was steady, but Claire had a hunch he wasn't quite as calm on the inside. He was simply trying to reassure her.

He continued to peruse the map, trying to look casual should the deputy glance over. His head was tilted toward the window to keep the deputy from getting a clear view.

"She's getting out," Alex said.

Claire's heart pounded. She didn't want to be discovered like this. Sopping wet, shivering, crouching in fear. She was as afraid for Alex and Mason as she was for herself. She'd never wanted to put anyone else in jeopardy. Especially Mason. Alex had chosen this. Mason had stumbled into it. He was innocent.

It seemed like an eternity before Alex said, "She's heading inside."

*Thank You, thank You, Lord*, Claire thought.

"Here comes Mason."

A few moments later the back passenger door opened. Mason slid a sympathetic look her way as he settled the dog food onto the floor next to Roscoe. He walked around the vehicle and quickly got in.

"Guess I should've parked on the other side of the building," he said, his tone droll.

"Just get us out of here," Alex said lightly.

Mason maneuvered out of the lot.

Once they were on the highway, Claire sat up again.

Mason used the rearview mirror to scan the road behind them. He caught Claire's eye and gave her a bright grin. "Looks to me," he said, "as if the good Lord is working overtime watching out for you today."

"Yes," Claire agreed, feeling an unexpected sense of peace. "He is."


Mason's single-level, ranch-style home was in a quiet neighborhood in a Portland suburb. The house was small, with only one bathroom and two bedrooms, but he was more than willing to share his space.

Alex was grateful because it was the ideal place to hide away. No one would be checking IDs, no one would be barging in to clean, no guests would be milling around. He didn't mind camping out on a strange couch again. He'd slept in far worse places over the years.

He and his friend were sitting at the kitchen table, warming up with cups of coffee. The aroma of the beef stew simmering in a Crock-Pot on the counter was making Alex ravenously hungry. He was thinking about dinner— in an effort to forget about the disastrous kiss he and Claire had shared—when Mason tossed him a verbal curveball.

"A guy I used to work with got a job with the Oakville PD," he casually stated.

Alex worked at keeping his expression even, though he was wondering where his friend was going with that bit of information. "Oh, yeah?"

"Anything you want me to try to find out for you?"

Alex hesitated.

Mason was young, one of the youngest on the team. He'd joined after a friend of his tangled with the wrong people. She hadn't lived to tell about it. He'd gone through the police academy right out of high school. Had served for a year, then had discovered HOPE, which he felt was more hands-on, and he'd never looked back.

"Look, I know who your friend is," Mason said bluntly. "I know she's accused of killing her husband, Jared Mitchell. I know you well enough to assume that if you're helping her, you have a good reason."

"I do," Alex agreed. "And yes, I'll take you up on your offer. If your contact is willing, I'd like to know how solid they think their case is against Claire. Also, I'd like to know if they have any other suspects."

"They're ready to charge her with murder," Mason said carefully. "I think that means they aren't looking at other suspects at this point."

"I need to know if the real murderer was ever on their radar."

"Real murderer," Mason echoed.

"Claire's innocent."

Mason said nothing.

"She's innocent," Alex repeated. "I'm going to help her prove it."

Mason winced. "You know that's the defense of just about every criminal ever, right?"

"Claire's not a criminal."

"How can you be so sure?"

"Because I know her."

"You know some murder suspect well enough to risk your neck trying to clear her name?" Mason sounded more curious than skeptical.

Alex didn't see any reason to keep Mason in the dark.

"I used to be engaged to her. Trust me. I know her. She's innocent."

Alex was met with a blank look while Mason tried to wrap his head around that information. After a moment he broke into a slow smile. "She's the one."

"The one what?" Alex demanded.

"The one that got away. The one that's turned you into a workaholic." Mason's head bobbed as he agreed with himself.

"She didn't get away," Alex said quietly. "I pushed her away."

Judging by the reaction to his kiss, she wasn't going to be reeled back into a relationship with him anytime soon. Possibly not ever. Did he even want a relationship with her? He thought maybe he did. Or were his emotions just running high due to the realization he had a daughter, compounded by the intensity of the situation they were in?

It didn't matter what he wanted. Because Claire had made it pretty clear how she felt about him. In that moment, he had thought she'd wanted him to kiss her. The way she'd felt in his arms, the way she'd been looking at him—

"If it was your fault, that's even worse," Mason continued, cutting into Alex's thoughts.

Alex tried to ignore him. "I wasn't there when she needed me before. I'm not bailing on her now. Jared's business partner, Xavier Ambrose, had Jared killed. We just need to prove it. What I'd like to know is whether or not the police have looked into him at any point."

"Xavier Ambrose, the guy you asked me to look into, was Jared Mitchell's business partner?" Mason's brow furrowed. "I didn't realize. I haven't had a chance to check him out yet. Helena has me working overtime trying to track a missing fifteen-year-old. I've been so buried in this case I've hardly had time for anything else. You think Xavier killed Jared?"

"Yes."

Mason seemed to mull that over. "I didn't realize you thought he was a murder suspect. I have a lead on the girl and Helena's thrown a few more cases my way. But I'll bump Xavier up on my list, look into his past just as soon as I can. In the meantime, I'll check with my contact at the department. It might take a few days for him to get back to me, but I'll see what I can do."

"Thanks. I appreciate it."

"No problem."

Claire wandered into the kitchen wearing the jeans and the cardigan she'd had on the night Alex had found her at the shack.

"Feel better?" Alex asked.

She nodded. "I'm warm and I'm dry. That definitely makes me feel better."

"Anyone hungry?" Mason asked. "I'm not much of a cook. I usually cook one big meal and spend the next few days eating it. I've got stew and bread from the bakery."

"Sounds delicious," Claire said. "What can I do to help?"

"You can set the table. You can find what you need there and there." He pointed to a cupboard and a drawer.

"Mason has a contact at the Oakville PD," Alex said as he began filling water glasses.

Claire paused with her hand on a stack of bowls. Her eyes were wide when she glanced over her shoulder at Alex. She quickly flicked her gaze to Mason.

"I hope French bread is okay with the stew. Rolls probably would've gone better." He turned to Claire as if still discussing nothing more pressing than dinner. "Yes, I know who you are. No, I'm not going to do anything about it. In our line of work—" he cast a glance at Alex "—situations often aren't what they seem. I trust Alex's judgment."

"Thank you," Claire said sincerely. She placed the bowls and spoons on the table and took a seat.

With hot pads, Mason carried the crock to the table and set it on a trivet. He returned to the counter for the bread.

Once they were all seated Mason said, "I'll lead grace, if you don't mind."

"Please do," Claire agreed.

"Dear Father, we thank You for the meal before us. We thank You for the friendship between us. I ask You to please watch over Alex and Claire on their journey. Please, let justice prevail. Amen."

"Amen," Alex and Claire echoed.

Alex caught Claire's eye. He could see that Mason's prayer touched her heart. It was a small gesture, but for a woman who felt as if the odds were stacked against her, it meant a lot.

They passed around the food and ate in silence for a few minutes.

"It's been so long since I've had a home-cooked meal," Claire said. "This is wonderful."

Mason chuckled. "Thanks. I know how to cook maybe five things. This is one of them."

"Then you're better off than I am," Alex admitted.

Mason was preparing a gibe when they were interrupted by Alex's phone.

"Excuse me," he said as he pulled it from his pocket. He frowned as Gretchen's name popped up. "Alex, here."

She wasn't put off by his brusque greeting. "I'd like your input on something."

"What's going on?"

"The house is being watched," Gretchen said. "There's been a car parked down the road, away from the gate, since I got here. Different car today, but same spot. I feel fairly confident they aren't planning on breaching the community. They're more of a nuisance than anything."

"Keeping an eye on who's coming and going," Alex decided.

Both Claire and Mason were blatantly eavesdropping. He didn't mind, he'd be sharing the information with them soon enough.

"I think so," Gretchen agreed.

Alex thought most likely they were watching for any sign of Claire. Xavier had to know that Beth was watching over Mia. Of course it would seem likely that Claire would want to see her daughter.

"I don't think they're a threat," Alex said. "I also don't think we should make it too easy for them. Why don't you give the local PD a call?"

"I was hoping you would say that. There's no law against parking on the street. But it would put it on law enforcement's radar that Beth's house is being staked out."

"That alone should raise at least a bit of suspicion," Alex said. Not that law enforcement could do much with it now. But perhaps it could help Claire's case later.

"I'll give them a call," Gretchen agreed.

"Everything else going okay?"

"Yes," she replied. "I haven't seen much of her husband, but Beth is very gracious. Her niece is a delight."

Alex was stabbed by an unexpected pang of jealousy. He wished he was the one watching over Mia right now.

"I trust you to take good care of them both."

"I know," Gretchen said. "You have nothing to worry about."

They disconnected. Alex slid his phone into his pocket. "That was Gretchen."

Claire leaned forward. "Is Mia okay?"

"She's doing fine. Gretchen called her a delight."

"So what's the problem?"

He reiterated the phone call.

Claire's shoulders slumped. "I hate that Xavier's men are that close to my daughter."

"Our daughter," Alex corrected.

Mason's eyebrows shot up but he was discreet enough not to address the comment.

"I don't like it, either," Alex admitted. "On the other hand, I think it'll only help your case. There's no way the police can miss the damage to the Jeep. Once Gretchen makes that phone call, they'll be aware that Beth's place is being staked out. Granted, Gretchen can't prove it's Beth's house that's being watched, but I have enough faith in your local PD to assume they'll put those two pieces of information together. To me, that's nothing short of suspicious."

"I think it's time we send the file on Xavier. We talked about it, but got sidetracked," Claire said.

"You have a file on the suspect?" Mason took a bite of stew as his curious gaze bounced between Alex and Claire.

"Yes," Alex answered. He filled Mason in on what they suspected the motive was, along with a summary of the information Claire had compiled.

"Dude," he said as he turned to Alex, "you really do need to get that information handed over. Now I see why you were wondering if they had any other suspects. Sounds like the guy could definitely have a motive."

"Mason has been swamped, but he's going to look into Xavier's past the first chance he gets," Alex told Claire.

"I'm working on a few other cases," Mason said to her, "but I'll make digging up some info on Xavier a priority."

"Maybe you'll discover the names of Xavier's henchmen," Claire said.

Mason's eyebrows shot up. "Henchmen?"

Alex told him about the gunmen at the shack, the meeting with Ruth and the car chase that ended with gunfire and a blown-out tire.

"As soon as they go over the Jeep," Mason said, "they'll see gun powder residue. That ought to raise a few questions."

"I can't run forever," Claire said quietly. "I'd like the case against Xavier to be as strong as possible before I turn myself in."

Alex didn't want to think about Claire turning herself in. He also didn't want to argue about it in front of Mason. He let the comment slide.

For now.

"What we need is solid proof," Alex told Mason. "We think he might've left something incriminating behind but going back to Claire's house is a huge risk. The police will be there in no time if we trip the alarm."

"So don't trip the alarm," Mason said.

Alex scoffed.

"No," Mason continued, "I'm serious. If you can get me enough information, I'm sure I can get you in."

"How?" Claire demanded, her curiosity clearly piqued. She looked to Alex for the answer.

He frowned. He wasn't happy to admit that he wasn't a techie sort of guy. He considered himself to have a fair amount of brains and his brawn had always come in handy. But knowledge of the ever-changing world of technology? Not so much. He'd always left that part to other people. Fortunately, Mason had the skills needed.

"There're a few ways a system can be hacked. I could disarm the alarm, but then the security company would probably take note of that," Mason explained. "I could also remotely set off the alarm."

"The point of that would be…?" Alex asked.

"In this case, it's probably not the best idea. But a few months ago it came in handy when we needed to get into that warehouse outside of Miami. We started setting off the alarm at random over the course of a few days. The security guys assumed there was a glitch in the system. When it was time for us to roll, we set it off again—their thugs blew it off and we caught them off guard. That probably won't work for you two. It might make law enforcement suspect that you're up to something."

"While this is all very interesting," Claire said politely, "I'm not sure how it's much help."

Mason grinned at her. "I'm getting to it. I could also suppress the system for you."

"Suppress the system?" Alex asked. He already liked the sound of that.

"Sure," Mason said. "I hack into the system, figure out what frequency it's using, the same way I would for remotely setting off the alarm. Instead of setting it off, I'd send in a signal that's stronger than that of the system and jam it. Then there's no activity between the sensor and the alarm. That way, when you go in, the alarm is overridden."

"Just like that?" Claire asked.

Mason shrugged. "For me? Yeah. I've been doing this for a while."

"Do you think that could work?" She rushed ahead

in excitement, answering her own question. "I think that could work."

"Of course it will work," Mason scoffed. "I can guarantee that I've gotten us into places with security far superior to whatever home alarm your husband had installed."

"Yeah," Alex said gruffly. "It would probably work."

Claire tilted her head, narrowing her eyes at him. "Why don't you sound happy about it?"

"There's still a whole lot of ways that plan could go sideways," he warned.

Mason shrugged. "I'm just throwing it out there. It'll give you two something to think about." He pushed his chair back. "You two can go relax while I clean up in here."

Claire shook her head. "You've done so much. Let me clean up."

"That's not necessary," Mason argued.

Claire stood and began gathering dirty dishes. "Please. My life has been in upheaval for weeks. You have no idea how much I'm craving normalcy. I love to putter around in the kitchen. It relaxes me."

Mason laughed. "Then by all means, make yourself at home and putter away."

Claire took Mason up on his offer. While he and Alex discussed operations at HOPE, she did the dishes, tidied the kitchen then poked around in his cupboards and pantry. She'd thought a batch of homemade brownies would be nice, but Mason didn't have cocoa powder. She settled on making oatmeal cookies after finding both oatmeal and raisins on the meagerly stocked shelves.

Baking calmed her but made her miss Mia terribly. She longed for the days when the two of them would mess up the kitchen together. Of course, she knew to always, always have it spotless by the time Jared had returned home. He deplored having anything out of order. Claire had learned that lesson the hard way.

"You've got a pretty comprehensive file started," Mason said as he strode into the kitchen. Alex appeared a moment later, clutching the binder.

Claire looped the dishtowel over the stove handle. "You went through it?"

"I did," Mason said.

"I was hoping looking the information over would give him a point of reference for when he begins his research," Alex said. "I also thought another pair of eyes on everything couldn't hurt."

"What do you think of the information?" Claire asked.

"I think you've got a great case against Xavier for smuggling. I suggest getting it turned into the detective on your case right away. Even if it doesn't immediately point to him as a murder suspect, it'll have the cops all over in his business for the time being."

"And that will give him less time to concentrate on going after you," Alex said.

Claire nodded. "If you have a scanner, I can start making copies. We could get them mailed off tonight."

Mason quirked an eyebrow at her. "No need to mess with that. I'll get them scanned and send a digital file straight to the detective on your case."

She frowned. "Can't they track that?"

Alex jabbed a thumb Mason's way. "Computer geek. Remember?"

Mason grinned. "Let's do this."

He took off toward the spare bedroom that doubled as his office. Claire and Alex followed.

Claire watched patiently as Mason fed page after page through his machine.

She had meticulously copied the papers documenting the black-market activity from Jared's file. The documents listed the item sold, the purchase date, the buyer's name and last—but possibly most crucial—the account number of an offshore bank account that Jared had suspected belonged to Xavier.

She had no doubt that Jared had compiled the information to serve himself but was grateful that he had. Additional pages documented the names of the smugglers Xavier worked with. Once the artifacts were in the country, he sold them through a phony auction house. Each item sold had a doctored history, masking the authentic origin.

When Mason was done scanning, she typed up a letter explaining the contents, including the fact that Jared was privy to the fraudulent activity. She signed her name because there was no reason not to. Mason attached it to the file, gave her one final assurance that the email address he used could not be tracked and then sent it off.

When the time came to turn herself in, she hoped the PD would have some sympathy for her if they understood why she'd gone on the run. She knew it was wishful thinking. She was breaking the law and they were not happy about it.

Once the file was scanned, they moved into the living room. Claire served cookies and coffee while Mason and Alex discussed her case.

"I could do some surveillance on your house," Mason told Claire when she joined them again. "If you two do decide to break in, it would be good to know if the area is being patrolled or whether it's being staked out by the police."

"It sounds like a good plan to me," Alex said.

If Alex and Mason thought so, Claire wasn't about to disagree.

"I think, from here on out," Alex said firmly, "you shouldn't leave Mason's house. Not until this is over. Now that they know you didn't skip the country, and it's been confirmed that you've been in the area, they'll intensify their search efforts."

"What you're saying is that you want to break into my house without me." Claire's eyebrows shot up as she silently dared him to try to refute her.

"It's not breaking in if you give me the key," Alex said, his tone light.

"I'm not sure the cops will feel the same way if you get caught." She shook her head. "It just doesn't feel right to have you at risk while I'm just sitting around."

"Claire." Alex placed his hand on her knee and gave her an imploring look. "I've been in sticky situations before. Lots of them. I can handle it."

"I don't doubt it." She gave his hand a firm squeeze, letting her fingers linger. "I just feel that I should be there. I obviously know my house better than anyone. It's a big house with a lot of rooms to cover. If I'm there, something might jump out at me."

"I'll let the two of you hash it out," Mason said. "I'm heading out in the morning, so if I'm going to do this, it has to be tonight." He rose from the couch and after a few last-minute instructions from Alex, he left.

Before Mason was even out of the driveway, Alex's phone buzzed.

"It's Gretchen." He got up and began to pace as he answered it.

Claire listened to the one-sided conversation, relieved when Alex didn't seem distressed.

When he disconnected he turned to her. "She was calling with an update. She said an officer stopped by. He talked to the men in the car. From what she could see, the officer wasn't able to do much. The car did leave."

"For now," Claire said.

"It will only look more suspicious if they come back." He paused. "Gretchen will keep an eye on the situation."

Claire was relieved that Alex thought Gretchen capable, but she wouldn't be content until Mia was once again in her care.

"I'm taking Mason to the airport tomorrow. You should have this in case you need to get in touch with me while I'm gone." He held a cell phone out to her. "It's the phone I tried to give to Ruth. I entered my number, Mason's and Gretchen's. I can't think of a circumstance where you might need any of the numbers but—"

"Erring on the side of caution is a good thing."

"Yes," Alex agreed. "It is."

# EIGHT

"Are you sure you don't want me to postpone this assignment?" Mason dropped his duffel bag by the front door. "I could go to the house with you, be a lookout, help search for whatever it is you're looking for."

"Thanks for the offer," Alex said, "but what we really need is that information on Xavier and you can dig that up from anywhere." Besides, should he and Claire happen to get caught, it would be best if Mason was out of the state. "As long as you get us into Claire's house when the time comes, we can handle the rest." He didn't want his friend to have any part of the actual break-in.

Mason had spent quite some time last night canvassing Claire's neighborhood. He had determined that a cruiser drove by at random intervals. It didn't appear that anyone—either Xavier's men or law enforcement—was staking the place out. When he'd returned, he'd started digging around in Xavier's past, but hadn't immediately come up with anything. Alex was confident that he would. He just hoped it was soon. He wanted to plead with his friend to rush the case along, remind him how urgent it was. The problem was that nearly every case Mason was hit with was urgent.

"I can't thank you enough for taking us in," Claire said.

"It's no problem," Mason replied. "Hopefully we'll meet again under better circumstances."

"I'd like that," she agreed.

"I'll let you know when I hear back from my contact at the department," he said.

"Hopefully a case against Xavier will build quickly now that they have the file on him," Alex said. He didn't plan on telling her that after he dropped Mason off at the airport, he was going to her house.

Last night Claire had given Mason the name of the security company, her internet carrier and her phone number. From there Mason had been able to track down the account. He'd played around in the system for a while to get a feel for it. Now they were good to go. Alex just needed to check in when he was ready so Mason could suppress the alarm at that time.

If Jared had left the insurance policy Ruth had spoken of, it had to be there. If Claire knew he was going, she'd insist on accompanying him.

He wanted her nowhere near the place. For a man who made a living by keeping his cool, he was sure getting fired up lately. The thought of Claire being in danger made his blood boil. He didn't want to contemplate that too deeply. They had a history. They had a child. Of course, he wanted her to be safe. It was as simple as that. His heated emotions did not have to mean that old feelings were threatening to take over.

"Do you have any idea what Jared could've stolen from Xavier?" Alex asked, trying to keep his head in the current conversation. "Did Jared bring anything home recently?"

Claire hitched up a shoulder. "The past several months Jared constantly brought items home. Any or all of his collection could've been stolen from Xavier."

"Did any piece stand out more than the other?" he wondered aloud. "If Jared stole something particularly priceless and Xavier wanted it back, that would also give him a motive. Was there anything Jared brought home that he kept hidden away? Maybe in his safe?" If there was, and it was missing, maybe they could prove that Xavier stole it back once Jared was out of the way.

"There wasn't much in his safe," Claire said, "other than large quantities of cash." She narrowed her eyes at him, as if wondering why he was pressing the matter now, when he was ready to walk out the door.

"I really should get going," Mason said as he grabbed his bag.

Alex hesitated. He was torn. He needed to drop Mason off at the airport so that he could have use of his vehicle while he was away. Yet he hated the idea of leaving Claire alone. Though it had only been a few days since they'd been reunited, they'd been incredibly intense days. He didn't like the thought of being separated from her. The airport would be far too busy, far too crowded, to risk allowing her to ride along.

The local news channel had featured Claire as their headline story the night before. They'd showed footage of the campground, overrun by law enforcement. The newscaster encouraged everyone in the area to check their property. It was mentioned that she was traveling with her dog and an unidentified male.

He'd used a fake ID at check-in, one he frequently used while on assignment. While working for HOPE it was often crucial to keep their identities secret to protect themselves from retaliation. He assumed that once they dusted the room for fingerprints, they'd identify him. The events of the past twenty-four hours suddenly made it feel as if they were up against an unknown deadline.

He didn't appreciate the feeling.

"I'll be fine," she assured him. "My phone is charged. I have Roscoe."

"I'll be back as soon as I can," he said.

Mason and Claire said their goodbyes. Alex followed Mason to the door but paused before stepping outside. He twisted back around, pulling Claire into a tight hug. She gasped in surprise but her arms flew around him, returning the gesture.

"I couldn't bear it if anything happened to you," he admitted. "Stay safe." He pressed a lingering kiss to her forehead, released her and took off after Mason.

It struck him that it had been a lot of years since he was hesitant to leave someone. In fact, the last time he'd felt so torn, he was also leaving Claire.

Discussion of Mason's latest assignment occupied the men for most of the drive. It wasn't until the airport was in sight that Mason swerved the conversation in another direction.

"I hope things work out for you and Claire," he said.

"Thanks. I think she'll be cleared soon."

Mason grinned. "Yeah, I hope that works out, too. What I meant was I hope things work out with *her*. You two obviously belong together."

Alex winced. "I think that ship has sailed. In fact, it sailed and it's been sunk."

"I don't believe that. You two are so in sync you finish each other's sentences. Dude, that kind of love doesn't come around often."

"I don't know." Alex shook his head. "I walked out on her."

"You did," Mason agreed. "And look at the length God went to leading you back to her. When has God ever led you astray? You're not going to let your pride stand in the way of His plan, are you?"

Alex didn't know what to say to that. Was Mason right? He had thought God had led him back into Claire's life to help her. Maybe even to make up for some of his past mistakes. Was His plan greater than that?

If it was, how was he going to make Claire see that? He didn't know if he could. Didn't know if he should even try. She had enough burden and worry resting on her shoulders right now. Would pressing the idea of a relationship only add to that?

Or would it have the opposite affect? Would the thought of a future together bring her the sort of happiness she'd been missing in her life?

Was he being selfish, thinking of that now, when her life was on the line?

Maybe he needed to rein his own growing feelings in. Deal with one issue at a time.

And right now, finding the real killer took precedence over anything else.

He pulled the truck up to the curb.

"Thanks for the ride. Gotta run," Mason said. "But you should remember one thing."

"What's that?"

"*Romans* 8:28." He slapped Alex on the shoulder and hopped out.

The verse echoed through Alex's mind. *And we know that all things work together for good to them that love God, to them who are the called according to his purpose.*

With those words, his mind went into another tailspin. Was resurrecting his relationship with Claire the good thing that might come out of this heartache? Was being a father, raising his daughter, all part of His plan?

Alex hoped so, but thinking of Claire's reluctance, he wasn't sure if Mason was right. While Claire thought his job was important, she couldn't live with his long absences. Yet he felt drawn to his work, as if the Lord was calling him to it. Could he explain that to Claire? Would it matter if he did?

Claire rinsed her glass in the kitchen sink before putting it in the dishwasher. She froze when a car door slammed. Roscoe was alerted to the arrival, as well. She heard his claws tap against the tile as he lumbered to the front door, his head tilted in curiosity.

There was no way Alex would be back yet. She hurried to the entryway. Through the frosted sidelights, she was barely able to make out a dark-clad figure approaching. She couldn't tell if it was a man or a woman.

Roscoe's tail began to wiggle. She grabbed his collar before his excitement became too intense.

Mason hadn't mentioned that he was expecting company. Did he have a cleaning lady? A friend with a key who stopped by to check on the place?

The washer and dryer were making a racket in the laundry room off the kitchen. She rushed to the machines to shut them off. She didn't want the noise to alert anyone to the fact that someone was in the house.

Roscoe wanted to investigate the arrival.

"Come here, boy." Her command was low but firm as she tugged him. She froze in the middle of the kitchen when the doorbell rang. Mason's house was small with not many places to hide. A bedroom closet would do, but she'd have to scamper through the entryway to get to that side of the house.

Though the sidelights were frosted, Claire worried the visitor would see her shadow.

As she tugged the dog across the kitchen she heard the doorknob jiggle. She frantically looked around. The only place to hide was the walk-in pantry. Last night's foray, searching for baking supplies, had proved the pantry was pretty bare. She opened the door and they both scooted inside. Keeping the light off, she crouched down next to the dog. She rubbed Roscoe's belly, hoping it would keep him distracted.

His body tensed when the front door closed with a thud. Her heart smacked against her rib cage in response.

She slid the cell phone from her back pocket, sending off a quick text to Alex.

Someone pulled into the driveway and now they're in the house. I don't know if they're alone.

She checked the volume and silenced the phone in case Alex got back to her. The light on the screen quickly blinked out, leaving her in darkness.

Her heart continued to knock around frantically when footsteps thudded across the kitchen floor.

Claire was sure the front door had been locked. Locked doors could be breached. Houses were broken into all the time.

Had a cop showed up? Probably not. He wouldn't let himself in. At least, no decent cop would. One of Xavier's men? Anything was possible. Her hands began to tremble. Mason hadn't warned that he'd been expecting anyone. However, any company, any visitor at all, posed a danger to her. Every person she ran across was a potential threat to her freedom. Anyone could recognize her, turn her in, condemn her to life behind bars. A life without her daughter.

If she was found, especially found cowering in a closet, it would raise suspicions. If she was recognized, she would be forced to bid her freedom farewell.

Mason had been so kind, so helpful. She didn't want to get him in trouble. And Alex. What would become of Mia if Alex was charged with aiding and abetting? Beth would take care of Mia, always. But it wouldn't be the same.

Her instinct told her it wasn't a cleaning lady. Mason wasn't the sort of man to forget details. He would've warned them if he was expecting someone.

Message alerts were off, but Claire's phone screen lit up.

On my way.

She wanted to ask him how long he would be. Had he left the airport already? Was he halfway home? Or was he still a good distance out? She didn't dare ask. Answering her text would only slow him down.

She used the lit screen to scan the pantry. The area was small, just barely large enough for her and Roscoe. Shelves lined two walls. There were no boxes, nothing to hide behind. Even if Alex was on his way, it could take him quite some time to return.

Roscoe's stubby tail began to wiggle again. She vigorously scrubbed at his muzzle, silently willing her ministrations to suppress his curiosity.

Claire strained her ears. The footsteps had receded. A door thudded closed. She couldn't be sure but thought it was the garage door. For a brief moment she contemplated bolting from the house. She and Roscoe could take refuge in the woods. The idea was quickly quelled. What if the intruder wasn't alone? What if someone was outside, circling the premises? She loathed feeling so helpless.

Satisfied that Roscoe was content, at least temporarily, she stood. Using the dim light of her phone screen, she maneuvered a frying pan off the top shelf. She cringed when it made a grating sound as it scraped against another pan. She froze for a moment, her ears straining. When she was sure she hadn't been heard, she lowered the pan to her side.

Roscoe seemed to tire of their circumstance. She felt him flop down at her feet, ready to nap. Claire eased herself closer to the door.

The garage door opened and closed again. This time the footsteps were accompanied by another sound. It took Claire a moment to realize something was being dragged across the kitchen floor. The thud of feet stopped directly in front of the pantry door.

*Please, Lord, keep me safe.*

Claire held the frying pan firmly in her grip.

It seemed ludicrous to think one of Xavier's men was in the house. She and Alex should be almost impossible to find. But she'd thought the same thing while hiding out in the hunting shack. All it had taken was one unfortunate, overheard phone call and the killers had tracked her down.

What if they'd been listening to a police scanner? What if they'd heard the call for an officer to check out the campground? It was possible they had spotted Alex and Claire scrambling out of the woods and into the truck.

Anything, she had learned, was possible.

Whoever was in the house lingered in the kitchen.

Were they taunting her?

Other than her heartbeat whooshing through her ears, there was silence.

A loud thud almost caused her to shriek. Roscoe leaped to his feet. The rushed scrabbling of his claws had sounded thunderous to Claire. She instantly dropped to shush him before he gave away their location for sure.

Intense grumbling erupted from the other side of the door. A scraping sound was reminiscent of something being lifted off the ground. A grunt, then the hollow echo of footsteps as the person left the room.

The front door closed with a bang.

She didn't move. She didn't trust that the person had really left. They could be skulking around, creeping up to the pantry this very second.

As Alex suggested, it was always better to err on the side of caution.

He was on his way. She would stay put until he reached her.


Alex constantly scanned the road as he pushed the speed limit. He didn't dare go too fast. He couldn't afford to be detained because he got pulled over. He had already dropped Mason off at the airport when Claire's text came in. He'd been halfway to her home when he'd whipped a U-turn to head back to Mason's.

He was hesitant to text Claire again. He trusted she was smart enough to hide. Most likely her phone was on silent. He wasn't going to take the chance if it wasn't.

Alex was used to operating under pressure. This time, it felt different. This time it was Claire who was counting on him. He wouldn't fail her.

*Please, God, keep her safe.*

It felt like an interminable amount of time had passed before Alex reached Mason's. He rolled into the driveway. A quick glance around confirmed there was no car. Hopefully whoever had arrived had left. Alone.

With gun in hand, he slid from the vehicle. The house

looked empty. The curtains drawn, just as they'd left them. The front door closed.

He tried the doorknob. Locked. He quickly slid in the key. When the door swung open he was greeted with silence. The house was as quiet as a tomb.

Was Claire here? Had the intruder taken her?

He moved down the hallway, checking out the bedrooms.

"Claire? Are you in here?" He said the words under his breath as he entered the guest bedroom. "It's Alex."

He tried Mason's bedroom, the bathroom, then headed back to the kitchen. He spotted a piece of paper on the center island. His heart catapulted. Was it a note? Surely it couldn't be a ransom note. He quickly closed the distance and scanned the paper.

Not a ransom note.

He breathed a sigh of relief.

"Claire?" His voice seemed to echo through the quiet house. "It's Alex. Are you here?"

He heard a soft *woof* and spun around.

The pantry door swung open. Claire emerged and threw herself at him.

"It's okay." He squeezed her into a hug. He was instantly reminded of how perfectly she had always fit in his arms. Her arms were tangled around his neck, her face buried in his chest. The feel of her sent his memory careening back in time. He was reminded yet again of how deeply he'd missed her.

When she let out a relieved sigh then lifted her face to his, she was so close he could see the golden flecks in her green eyes, feel her breath on his cheek.

Their gazes locked and then Claire took a step back and slid from his arms. They felt empty without her. He wanted to reach for her, to reel her back in. Every cell in his body suddenly ached with missing her over the years. He considered telling her so, but when she crossed her arms over her stomach in a protective stance he lost his nerve.

"Someone was here," she said. "Are you sure they're gone?"

He cleared his throat. "It was Mason's sister. She stopped by to borrow his tent. She left a note on the counter."

"A tent?" Claire glanced at the counter where the note still sat. "That makes sense. It sounded like whoever was here went into the garage. She was dragging something and must've dropped it at one point."

"I'll have to check in with Mason when he lands," Alex said. "I wonder if we need to be concerned about any more unexpected guests dropping by."

"In the meantime," Claire said, "I want to drive by my house."

Alex clenched his jaw. Her request didn't surprise him.

"For what reason, exactly?" he asked. "You know it's dangerous for you to be in the vicinity."

"I understand that," she said calmly, "but I know my neighborhood better than anyone. I know Mason checked it over. However, I want to see it for myself. He didn't think anyone was staking the area out. Maybe they're not. Maybe we can sneak in tonight. At the very least, I think it would benefit you to drive through the neighborhood. I know you want to go through Jared's office as soon as possible. But wouldn't it help to know the layout?"

She was right. That was why he'd planned on driving through on his way back from the airport, maybe even breaking in right then, depending on the feel he had for the situation. His plans were thrown for a tailspin. He'd planned on going *alone*.

"Claire, we've been over this. It's too dangerous for you."

"It's not any more dangerous for me than for you," she argued. "Like it or not, you're aiding and abetting."

"I'm willing to take the risk."

"So am I."

Alex ground out a frustrated sigh. How could he have forgotten how stubborn this woman could be? Well, she wasn't the only one. He wasn't willing to budge on this. Allowing Claire to drive through her old neighborhood would be dangerous.

He pivoted, turning to leave the kitchen.

"Where do you think you're going?" she demanded.

He held up a hand to halt further protest. "I'm going to grab something from the other room. I'll be right back."

Mason's spare laptop was sitting on his desk in the guest room. Alex grabbed it and headed back to the kitchen. By the time he returned, Claire had turned on the small television that rested on the countertop. She was flipping through the channels when Alex walked in. He had to assume she was looking for a local news station. She lowered the volume when she spotted him.

"What are you doing with that?" she asked as she crossed the room to the table.

"Driving past your house is probably out of the question." *Especially since you insist on coming along*, he added silently. He settled the laptop on the table and fired it up. "I thought this would be the next best thing. It's crazy what you can find on the internet."

Less than five minutes later Alex had loaded an aerial map of Claire's neighborhood. He zoomed in, scrolling past each home as Claire gave him a rundown of her neighbors. Lastly, Alex zeroed in on her house and the area immediately surrounding it.

The backyard couldn't be seen from the road. A thin copse of trees encircled the home on three sides. It would've been easy for an intruder to reach the pool area without being spotted by neighbors once the sun had set.

"The trees could work in our favor," Alex said. "They'd provide cover for us." He didn't intend to take Claire along, but including her now delayed arguing about it. "Unfortunately they'd provide cover for anyone watching for us."

"I was thinking the same thing," she agreed. "But what choice do we have?" She pointed to the house directly south of hers. "The Hendersons moved to California. Their house is empty. You can't see it from the road."

Alex wasn't sure he liked where she was going with this.

"We could park in the Henderson's driveway, out of the way, walk through the woods and check out Jared's office."

It sounded like a reasonable plan. In fact, it was the plan he would've come up with himself if given a few moments to think it over.

However, as far as he was concerned, the plan had one major flaw. He still thought it was too risky for Claire to join him. He knew she'd be too stubborn to see it that way.

"Mason still needs time to look into Xavier's past," Alex said in an effort to stall. He still hoped to sneak away and inspect the house on his own. She'd be furious. He could deal with furious, as long as she was safe. "Maybe we should wait to see what he has to say."

He could feel Claire's gaze boring into him. He didn't dare look her way, afraid she'd know what he was planning.

"Sure."

Alex heard the suspicion in her tone. He wasn't foolish enough to think a subject change would deter her but thought it would get him off the hook temporarily.

"You know what would be helpful?" he asked.

She hoisted an eyebrow in question.

"If you could draw out the floorplan of both the upper and lower level," he said. "That way I'll have an idea of where I need to go."

"Sure," Claire agreed. "I can do that."

"If you don't mind me asking," he began as he leaned back in his chair, "how did you and Jared meet? I don't want to offend, but it doesn't seem to me that you had much in common." He knew Claire wasn't the sort of woman to be swayed by a big bank account or a fancy house.

"Beth helped organize a charity ball a few years ago. It was to raise money to update the pediatric wing of the hospital her husband works at. Of course, I had to go. I wanted to support Beth, and it was for a good cause." Claire paused, as if lost in her memories of that time. "I was content to go without a date. However another woman on the planning committee asked Beth if I'd be willing to attend with Jared. Her husband had done business with him and she hoped he'd make a sizeable contribution. He had just returned from an extended business trip and didn't have a date for the evening."

"I read an article stating that he was a very generous man."

"He liked to throw money around. I agreed to go with him, after Beth twisted my arm. She was convinced he'd be more generous if he had a date to impress." Claire pressed out an exasperated sigh. "I had been dreading the evening but was surprised to find that he was very charming. Throughout dinner we discussed different charities we'd been involved with. I was impressed by him. Looking back, I think the conversation was scripted. I've learned Jared was adept at putting on a front for whomever he was trying to impress. Regardless, when he asked me out on a date the following weekend, I agreed."

"You didn't date long," Alex pointed out.

"No. We didn't. I naïvely thought I was at a point in my life where I knew what I wanted. I thought he was it. I thought he'd provide stability and companionship," she said quietly. "While we were dating, everything seemed so perfect."

"Too perfect?"

"Looking back, I suppose so."

Alex had wanted to distract Claire. He hadn't wanted to upset her. She sounded anything but happy as she discussed her marriage to Jared. Not that he could blame her, but he had been curious. He was also curious about Jared's relationship with Xavier.

"How did he and Xavier become business partners?"

"They were partners long before Jared and I met," Claire explained. "They had been acquaintances for years. One night they got talking after a golf game at the country club. Xavier knew of a hotel chain that was selling out. He wanted to buy into it but was looking for an investor. Jared was interested, but only if he could be an equal partner."

"And the rest is history," Alex guessed.

"Yes," Claire agreed. "That about sums it up. He—"

She froze, her gaze zeroed in on something over his shoulder.

Alex swiveled around as she leaped from her chair. She hurried to the small television. She reached for the volume and turned it up, but not before Alex caught sight of what had upset her.

Both of their faces were plastered across the screen.

Alex clenched his jaw as the news report blasted out of the speakers.

"—traveling with a long-time acquaintance. Alex Vasquez, a Portland native, has extensive military training. They are believed to be armed and dangerous. If you spot this couple, do not approach them or try to apprehend them. Call 9-1-1 immediately."

A commercial for a local car dealership followed. She flipped the television off mid-advertisement.

"Alex…" Claire's tone was regretful, as was her pain-filled expression.

"It's okay," he said sincerely. He stood, crossed the room and pulled her into his chest. She didn't resist as he held her close. "I knew what I was getting myself into. If I had it to do over again, I'd still show up at the shack in a heartbeat."

# NINE

The night Alex ran back into her life, he'd told Claire he'd known she hadn't killed Jared because he knew her. Claire had wanted to tell him it worked both ways. She knew him, too. Knew him well enough to know he was planning something. She could sense it. She could almost hear the cogs of his mind turning, churning out a plan.

One that he, no doubt, intended to keep from her.

Common sense told her it revolved around sneaking into her house.

As they worked side by side in Mason's kitchen, preparing dinner, she pretended to be oblivious. If she asked him point-blank, she thought he'd probably deny it. That was only part of the reason she didn't mention it.

She didn't want him to know she was onto him. It would be easier to keep an eye on him that way.

"Have you given any thought to what you're going to do once your name is cleared?" Alex asked.

Claire appreciated his optimism.

She continued to chop veggies for a salad while Alex stood, hip propped against the countertop, keeping an eye on the spaghetti sauce.

"I have," she admitted. "I'm hoping to sell the house." She couldn't imagine living there. The house had never really suited her. Now she couldn't imagine staying in the place where Jared had died. It held too many awful memories.

"And then?" he prodded. "Do you plan on staying in the area?"

She slid her pile of tomatoes into a bowl and reached for a cucumber. "Yes. If you're wondering because of Mia, you have nothing to worry about. I'm not sure if I'll stay in Oakville or if we'll move to another Portland suburb. Regardless, I won't be taking her far."

"I appreciate that. I *was* wondering because of Mia, but I'm also concerned about you. I know you like stability. The last month has been anything but." He moved away from the counter, went to the cupboard and began pulling out dinnerware.

The unexpected feeling of domesticity hit her hard. In the past she had loved sharing day-to-day tasks with Alex. Whether it be an evening of cooking, a week of re-painting their apartment or an afternoon rearranging fur-niture. They had made such a good team. Even the most tedious of tasks had been enjoyable with Alex by her side.

She craved the simplistic normalcy of it all.

Her life with Jared had been so vastly different from her life with Alex.

Alex caught her gazing at him as she reached for a red pepper. It wasn't the first time he'd caught her. Truth be told, she was pretty sure she'd spied him looking at her a time or two, as well. She couldn't let herself think about what those looks might mean.

His lip quirked up in a half smile. She valiantly tried to convince herself that her heart hadn't skipped a beat. She lowered her gaze and willed herself to concentrate on the vegetables.

Alex was Mia's father. He would always be a part of

Claire's life because of the shared connection. However she knew how seriously he took his work. Right now, she knew he thought of her as an assignment. Once she was out of danger, he would lose interest in her again.

She jumped when his hand covered hers, stilling the knife. She glanced up at him, surprised by the serious expression he wore.

"I'm anxious to meet my daughter," he said sincerely. "I want you to know that I intend to be a part of her life. I have three years to make up for. I don't want to miss out on any more time with her."

His hand slid away and he took a step back. He studied her face, anxious to hear her thoughts on the matter.

"I'm happy to hear that. She needs her father." She set the knife down and turned to face him fully. "I have to admit, I do have my concerns. I assume your career takes you out of town for long stretches at a time." A muscle ticked in his jaw, confirming her suspicion. "I understand your work is important to you. It should be. It sounds as though the organization is saving lives. However, I need to know that Mia will be a priority in your life. If you make promises to her, I expect you to keep them. If you tell her you'll be there, you had better be. If I'm going to allow you to get close to her, she needs to feel like she matters to you. I don't want her to feel like an afterthought."

He nodded. "I understand. I know you couldn't rely on me toward the end of our relationship. For that, I'm sorry. Things will be different with Mia. I promise you."

"I needed to hear that."

"My job is flexible. I can turn down assignments if I need to."

"You could turn down security-detail assignments when we were engaged. But you never did." There was no rebuke, only a gentle reminder in her tone. She had no doubt that Alex wanted to be a good father. But he was going to have to prove himself to her.

"One of the many mistakes I made in the past."

"I need you to know I'm not dragging up the past out of spite," she said.

"I know. You're not that kind of person."

"I have Mia's feelings to consider and I won't do anything that could hurt her."

He moved forward and reached for her hands again. "I understand. I always knew you would make an amazing mother. I simply want the opportunity to be a good father."

"I miss her," she said miserably. "I truly think leaving her with Beth was for the best. But I miss her so much. I'm trying so hard not to be angry. Sometimes it creeps up on me. When I'm not angry, I'm afraid. I'm trying to trust in God and I hate that I can feel my faith wavering. What if He doesn't get me out of this?"

Her lower lip began to tremble. She didn't want to cry. Not here. Not now. Not in front of Alex. He was always so strong. In the past, she had counted on that strength, leaned on it. She no longer had a right to it.

"He will get you through this." Alex wrapped his arms around her, cocooning her against his chest. He felt wonderful yet frightening. She was afraid that she was sliding along a dangerous path. It would be all too easy to fall for him. Fall hard. She'd done it before and she should be smart enough not to do it again.

She wasn't feeling smart.

She was feeling scared and alone.

His nearness offered comfort she hadn't felt in such a long time. Her tension eased as her body melted into his. Being near him felt so natural. It made her nostalgic, longing for the days when their love was solid and secure.

She had thought she'd moved past missing him.

As she soaked up his nearness, her heart rattled painfully as she thought of him leaving again. And he would leave. It was inevitable. She knew she needed to guard her heart. She knew it wasn't her imagination that they were growing close again. She couldn't let that happen. Couldn't let herself get any more attached than she already was.

It would only end in heartache.

"I'm here to help you through this, too," he murmured.

His words reminded her of exactly *why* he was there. She placed her hands against his chest and stepped back. He was there because she was in trouble. He was intent on rescuing her. Nothing more, nothing less.

"I should check the sauce." Claire shrugged out of his embrace, turning away from him.

"You do that," Alex agreed. "I thought of something I need to do."

Claire glanced over her shoulder on her way to the stove. "Right now?"

"I can't think of a better time. I'll be right back."

He sauntered out of the kitchen, leaving Claire staring at his back. It wasn't like Alex to walk away from a conversation. Or maybe his emotions were as tangled as hers and he needed a moment to himself.

She stirred the sauce, drained the noodles and set them both on the back burners.

He returned to the kitchen in the midst of a phone call. An unexpected glint in his eye took her by surprise. Had one of his or Mason's contacts come through? Did she dare hope?

Before she could ponder the thought too deeply, he was standing in front of her.

"Someone wants to speak with you."

He pressed the phone to her ear. Her hand slid over his as she held the phone in place.

"It's Gretchen," he whispered.

"Hello?" She shot him a questioning look as he backed away.

"Hello, there." Gretchen's voice was melodic. She sounded young. Too young to be in the line of work she was in. "I don't think this is the best idea, so I'd like you to keep it short."

Claire didn't have a chance to question her. A moment later a familiar voice floated across the line, making her knees go weak.

"Momma?" Mia's tone held equal parts happiness and curiosity. "Momma, is it you?"

Claire collapsed into the kitchen chair, grateful that it was there. "Hi, baby." Her voice caught in her throat.

Claire felt Alex watching her. She looked up and caught his eye. His expression was indecipherable. Perhaps it was a look of peace melded with a bit of longing. She quickly activated the speakerphone option.

"I miss you," Mia announced.

Her small, warm voice wrapped around Claire's heart, bringing a burst of pleasure to her day.

"I miss you, too," she said.

"I can't go to the park anymore but Auntie got a swing set."

"Did she?"

"Yes! It has a slide and a castle because I'm a princess!"

Claire watched as Alex scrubbed a hand over his face, as if trying to mask his emotions. Claire had to assume this wasn't the introduction to his daughter that he had longed for, but it was touching to watch his reaction all the same.

They listened as Mia prattled on about nonsensical things such as Popsicles and unicorns, and then moved on to the new doll buggy Beth had given her. She smiled as their daughter complained about string beans and oat-meal.

She let her gaze fall away from Alex, closed her eyes and soaked up the few precious moments she had with her child.

Mia spoke quickly, excitedly, as she confessed every grievance and delight that flowed into her mind. It was as if she'd saved it all up for this very phone call.

Claire listened, cherishing every word, content to hear the sound of her daughter's voice.

The little girl finally paused long enough to ask, "When are you coming home?"

*Soon.* Claire wanted to say soon. She wouldn't lie, though.

"I don't know, baby. I have some work to do. I wish I could be with you right now, but I can't."

"I don't like you to be gone." Mia's excitement had flipped to a full-blown pout.

"I don't like it, either." She pulled in a breath, knowing the call had to come to an end soon. "I want you to remember that I love you. I love you so much."

"I love you, too, Momma."

A background voice melded with Mia's. "Time's up," Gretchen said.

"'Bye!"

"'Bye, Mia."

The line disconnected. Claire sat utterly still, trying to freeze time, trying to remember the sound of her daughter's voice, of every word that was spoken. She clenched the silent phone, trying to pull the moment back.

She had to choke down a sob when reality sank in. The call was over. The tenuous connection to her daughter had ended for now. Speaking with her had been pure joy but the silence left a vast cavern of sorrow in its wake.

"I'm sorry." Alex had moved so he was kneeling in front of her. His hands rested on her knees. "Was that a bad idea? Did it make missing her worse? I didn't want to make it harder for you."

"You didn't." She knew she wasn't alone in her heartache. Alex didn't even try to hide that hearing his daughter for the first time tore at his heart. "I'm sure that couldn't have been easy for you."

His lips quirked up in a sad smile. "It wasn't but I'm glad you put her on speakerphone. I wouldn't have wanted to miss that for anything."

Claire refused to let herself cry. Too many tears had been shed already. "I want to get my life back," she said, her tone fierce.

"You will," Alex assured her. "Once this is over, you're going to have the life you always wanted."

He hesitated, and Claire sensed he had more to say. She tilted her head to the side and waited him out. She was hit by a wave of disappointment when he gave her knee a squeeze, rose to his feet and let the conversation fade away.

Alex tucked the edge of the blanket into the couch, tossed his pillow onto it then dropped into a chair on the other side of the room. He was far too wired to sleep. He braced his elbows on his knees, placed his face in his hands and let out a frustrated breath.

Hearing his daughter's voice for the first time had hit

him in a way he hadn't been prepared for. Until that moment the thought of having a daughter had seemed abstract, still so very hard to grasp. But once he'd heard her voice, it was as if her little fingers had wrapped themselves around his heart.

Claire had agreed to let him be a part of Mia's life. But how much of a part? Would it be enough? Would anything other than being a full-time father suffice? He didn't think it would. As he sat there, his mind spinning, he realized he wanted so much more than that. He wished he could go back in time, make things right. He wished they could be a happy family.

He didn't see that happening. Not now. Claire had shied away from his kiss. Had ducked out from his embrace. Sometimes he thought she looked at him as if her feelings mirrored his growing attraction. But then she'd hit him with a dose of reality. She'd pull away from him, reminding him that he had no right to her and she no longer had an interest in him.

"Alex?"

He snapped his head up, surprised to see Claire standing in the doorway. The sight of her sent the familiar sense of longing coursing through him. She was so beautiful. Not just on the outside. Claire was the strongest, most caring woman he'd ever met. Leaving her had been the worst decision he'd ever made. He hated thinking of the time when he'd have to leave her again.

She tugged her cardigan around her waist and said, "I was going to get a glass of water. I saw you sitting there. Are you okay?"

"I'm fine," he said automatically.

She wandered into the living room, gingerly settling onto the only other chair in the room. "Are you sure?" she pressed.

He nodded then sighed. "Maybe. Maybe not. I was thinking of Mia."

She nodded, silently encouraging him to go on.

"I don't think I can settle for being a part-time dad. I have a lot of years to make up for. I missed out on so much. I'm not willing to miss out on anything more."

Claire's expression became guarded. "What are you saying? Are you asking for joint custody? I don't think that's a good idea. Raising a child is an extraordinary commitment. Commitment is not exactly your strong suit."

He winced, knowing he probably deserved it, but the words still stung.

"I'm not the person I used to be Claire. Things happened, things you aren't aware of. I've changed. I've got my priorities straight now."

She was silent for a long while, mulling over what he'd said. Finally her expression softened. "You do seem different. More like your old self, the way you were when we first met," she said. "Tell me what happened."

"I was attacked. Stabbed," he said, absently placing his hand on his abdomen.

"'Stabbed'?" Claire echoed, eyes widening in shock. "How badly were you hurt?"

Alex hesitated then plunged ahead, knowing Claire deserved the truth. "Pretty badly. I lost a lot of blood. I almost didn't pull through."

She let her gaze fall to the floor, unable to look him in the eye. "How did it happen?"

He thought of the gang that had gotten the jump on him in an alley. He'd gotten separated from his team and it had taken them precious minutes to catch up to him. "A rescue attempt got a little rocky."

"*Rocky?* Is that how you would describe it?" She

blinked quickly, as if trying to stave off tears. "You almost died."

"Hey, it happened a couple years ago," he said gently. "I'm fine."

"You admitted you almost weren't." Her voice was raspy and it tore at his heart. "It sounds as if you're fortunate to be alive."

"I told you," he said, "God heard your prayers. You asked Him to keep me safe. He did. I pulled through."

"I hate that you're so reckless with your life." She shook her head. "I know you blamed yourself for the lives that were lost in the bombing but being careless with your life isn't going to bring the others back."

"I know."

Claire had told him this so many times before. In the past, he'd heard her words but he hadn't accepted their truth.

"I think it's time we had a little talk." He dragged a hand through his hair, taking a moment to pull his thoughts together. "The injury changed my life in a lot of ways."

He knew Claire was listening, even though she wasn't looking at him. Her hands were folded firmly in her lap. She was so tightly wound she looked like she could fly to pieces at the slightest provocation. The scar he now bore symbolized her worst fear.

"When I came out of surgery, a chaplain came to see me," he began. "He asked me who he could call. You know what my answer was?"

She lifted her eyes to his.

"No one," Alex replied. "I had *no one* for him to call."

"You could have called me," Claire said. "I would've been there for you."

"I know." She would've, he knew, because that was

the sort of person she was. Kind, caring, generous to a fault. "But it would've been unfair of me to ask. He visited with me on and off the next few days. He talked to me about God's forgiveness, His mercy. His unending love. When I was released from the hospital I was put on leave. I spent more time at my apartment than I have before or since. During that time, I did a lot of soul searching. A lot of Bible reading. The chaplain had visited me every day until I was sent home. He opened my eyes to the irony of what I was doing. It didn't happen overnight, but eventually I realized how backward I had everything. I work so hard to reunite families. I work with people who would give *anything* to get back family members who have been taken from them. But me? I walked away from you, the person who was the most important to me."

Claire's voice wobbled when she said, "I still don't understand why you thought you had to leave."

How did he explain it to her when he didn't entirely understand it himself? There wasn't just one reason. It was a culmination of everything going on in his head, in his life, at the time. He knew he had to try. He owed her at least that.

He didn't like to think about those dark days, but he had to go back to that time, to that place in his mind. It was the only way he could adequately explain his actions to Claire.

"After I left the military, I was so angry about what happened. I felt so much guilt. I blamed myself, thinking there had to have been *something* that I should've done differently," he began. "Memories of the bombing of the school consumed me. I'd seen death before, but not of that magnitude. I was on lookout, far enough away that I wasn't injured by the explosion. But I saw the aftermath." A suicide bomber had entered the building. One of the teachers that Alex and his team were familiar with, someone they had thought was safe. They'd been wrong. And innocent lives had paid the price. "I felt worthless. I felt unworthy of being alive. I felt unworthy of *you*."

"You were never unworthy of me," she said firmly. "That doesn't make sense."

"Not much about death and war does make sense," he argued. "I don't know how to explain it other than to say that I was in a real dark place in my life. I didn't know God the way I do now. You tried so hard to be understanding, to be patient, and that just made it worse."

She leaned forward, tears glistening in her eyes. "How? How did I make things worse?"

"I felt so undeserving of you. I felt like such a failure." He got up and began to pace. "You were this bright light, but I knew you were becoming frustrated with me. Not that I blame you. I was withdrawn, angry—"

"And hurting," Claire said. "You were hurting."

He nodded. "Yes. I was. I was also reckless, just as you said. I think I felt so much guilt over being alive when so many others had died, that I figured if I didn't make it out of my next assignment, I was only getting what I deserved. But you? You deserved so much better than what I could give you."

"Do you still think you did the right thing?"

He blew out a weary sigh. "I honestly don't know how to answer that. I think—given the emotional state I was in—if I'd stayed, our relationship would've continued to crumble. You might have ended up resenting me." She looked as if she were about to argue so he quickly pushed ahead. "What I can say is that I am truly sorry for leaving the way I did. I'm sorry for hurting you. I'm sorry for leaving you alone. I'm sorry for not being there for Mia."

"I was always afraid for you," Claire said. "When you came back from Afghanistan, you were so different. You shut down and you completely shut me out."

Alex thought Mason was right. God had led him back to Claire for a reason. She needed the honesty he hadn't been able to give her before.

"There's been no one since you. I just thought you should know." He met her gaze, noted the surprised look in her eyes. "No one could replace you. There was nothing missing in our relationship. You gave of yourself so freely, so completely. I felt like I could give nothing in return. I was worn out, empty. When I left, it was because of me. Something in me was broken, missing. My life was on a downward spiral and I was afraid of dragging you down with me."

Her lip quivered, tears shimmered in her eyes. "I felt like I wasn't enough for you."

"I never meant for you to feel that way." The pain etched across her features cut into him, too. In trying to protect her, he'd hurt her worse than he'd imagined.

For a few hours he'd allowed himself to toy with the idea Mason had put in his head. He'd thought about creating a new life with Claire and their daughter. Seeing how deeply her hurt still ran, he decided he had best put that fanciful thinking aside. Claire wasn't with him right now by choice but simply out of necessity.

She hesitated before saying, "What happens the next time a mission goes wrong? What happens when you lose someone? Are you going to shut Mia out?"

"It's happened. I've learned to cope. I've realized I can't save everyone. Only He has control over that." He dropped onto the chair again, feeling exhausted by the conversation. "For so long I fought that. I felt as if I just needed to try harder. Put more hours in. I thought it was about me. But it's not. It's about Him. I finally handed all of my fears, my insecurities, over to Him. I still strive to do my best, but I've accepted that there's a whole lot that's out of my control."

She sighed as she hoisted herself from the chair. "I hope so, Alex. For your sake and Mia's, I truly hope so."

She left the room without another word and Alex was left alone with his regrets.

# TEN

As Claire sat alone in the kitchen, she felt smothered by the dismal atmosphere of the house. Clouds had been dumping rain all day. It pattered against the windows incessantly.

It did nothing to boost her mood. She'd slept intermittently the night before. In part because she worried Alex would run back to her old neighborhood without her and in part because their conversation needled at her.

Had he changed as much as he said he had? Had he really and truly accepted Christ into his life? It seemed to her that he had. His demeanor was calmer and he seemed more at peace. And so very anxious to spend time with his daughter.

His apology meant the world to her. It was an apology she'd never thought she'd receive. She'd known how badly Alex had struggled trying to come to terms with what he'd seen while deployed. It didn't surprise her that only God had been able to settle Alex's heart and give him some peace.

Last night the heart-to-heart they'd had reminded her of how close they used to be. To know that he hadn't been interested in another woman since her caused a swirl of mixed emotions. Did it mean that a piece—even if it was a small piece—of his heart still belonged to her? She didn't know. She wasn't sure what to do with that information, other than to mentally file it away to think about later. Until she was cleared of murder charges, it would be silly and reckless to think about the possibility of reuniting with Alex.

She wanted him to be a part of Mia's life, but she hated the idea of having to share her, of allowing Alex to take Mia on occasion. There would be so many details to work out. So many ways for things to get complicated.

Not that they could get much more complicated than they already were.

She sat at the kitchen table with her third cup of coffee and Mason's laptop. Reading about the ongoing search effort to track her and Alex down made her stomach queasy. Alex had sequestered himself away in the spare bedroom. At first, she'd assumed he was avoiding her. Eventually she realized he was working. The mellow timbre of his voice floated through the door and down the hallway. When he'd come into the kitchen for his own refill of coffee, he told her that a few of the new team members he'd been mentoring needed advice. He was able to continue his mentorship from afar.

She was happy at least one of them was being productive. She flipped the laptop closed. It was unbearable, reading the ridiculously untrue and unkind things that were being said about her. The media painted Jared out to be a devoted husband and Claire as the unstable wife.

"Are you done with the laptop?"

She glanced up to find Alex leaning against the kitchen's door frame. His arms were crossed over his chest. His sculpted biceps were prominently displayed courtesy of his short-sleeved T-shirt. He looked invincible, but she knew that wasn't true. Life was fragile and so very precious. The scar he now bore was irrefutable proof of that.

She realized he was looking at her with raised eyebrows and remembered he'd asked her a question.

"Yes, sorry. I'm done."

"I just got off the phone with Mason," Alex said.

"Did he find something useful?" She was almost afraid to hope.

"He thinks he might have. He sent a file to the email I use for HOPE. It's more secure than your average account. If you're not using the laptop, I'd like to take a look."

"Please." Claire slid the computer across the table to the empty seat. "I think I could use more coffee. Would you be interested if I make another pot?"

"Definitely." Alex didn't look up as he spoke. His fingers were already flying over the keyboard, logging into his account.

Claire moved to the counter. She didn't necessarily need more coffee, she simply couldn't bear to sit still. While she busied herself rinsing out the carafe, Alex studied the screen.

Once the new pot was brewing, she settled back into her seat.

A grim smile settled onto Alex's face. "He has a past all right."

Claire waited, her eyes on Alex as he finished reading.

"Do you want to read it yourself?" he asked.

"Just tell me," she requested. Her hands were shaking. Mason had found something on Xavier. But was it enough? Would it be enough to cast doubt on the man?

"Are you aware of how Xavier amassed his wealth?"

Claire tilted her head to the side, wondering what he

was getting at. "He comes from a wealthy family. At least, that's what Jared said."

"In his youth his name was Todd Cushman. He was often in trouble as a juvenile. He grew up on the streets of Chicago, was involved with a gang. He did some time in juvie for theft. The worst of it was a gang-related fight. He nearly beat a rival gang member to death. Fortunately for him, the kid survived."

Claire released the breath she hadn't realized she'd been holding hostage. "Aren't juvenile records sealed?"

Alex gave her a pointed look. "I told you, Mason is good at what he does."

The coffeepot stopped sputtering and she rose to retrieve filled mugs.

"It doesn't paint a very nice picture of his past," Claire said as she poured. "How in the world did he go from being a gang member to what he is now?"

"When Xavier was seventeen, his uncle George came into the picture. George was Xavier's maternal uncle. He was originally from Chicago. Xavier beat the odds, got out and became a self-made millionaire. According to Mason, George was quite the philanthropist."

"The perfect person to take in a troubled youth," Claire said.

"It appears so. Xavier had gotten himself into quite a bit of trouble selling narcotics." Alex's eyebrows scrunched. "According to Mason's notes, it appears Xavier never used. He was arrested for various crimes, but his drug tests always came back clean."

"He was just a dealer, staying clean and clearheaded while he made money off the vices of others." Claire shook her head as she placed the two mugs of coffee on the table.

Alex continued, "George cut a deal with the judge. He

agreed to take full responsibility for Xavier if he was released to his custody after another short stint in juvie for the knifing incident. The judge allowed it—after George agreed to get him counseling. George moved Xavier to Portland. On the surface it appears that Xavier turned his life around."

"On the surface?" She supposed she should be happy that Xavier had turned his life around, but that didn't help her case much. Xavier was older than Jared had been. He was nearing forty. Had he really spent the last two decades being the upstanding citizen he appeared to be? Well, other than working the black market and murdering her husband?

"Shortly after Todd came to live with George, he changed his name to Xavier and took George's last name."

"That makes sense," Claire said quietly. "He probably wanted a clean start."

"He got it, all right. A clean start, a brand-new life. Seven years after moving in with his uncle George, George died in a freak boating accident. Xavier was his sole heir. He inherited his uncle's business holdings along with his millions."

Claire's eyebrows shot up. "What sort of freak boating accident?"

"He was bass fishing up at Silver Lake in Washington. Apparently he was alone and fell out of the boat. He drowned. There were no witnesses. The boat was anchored and discovered by fishermen in the morning. Divers found his body the next day."

"Drowned." A feeling of nausea cascaded through Claire. "Like Jared."

"Entirely different situation," Alex said quietly, "with the same result."

"Why was it suspicious?"

"George was an expert fisherman. Some guys golf, some guys play tennis, but fishing was his sport of choice. He'd won several fishing tournaments. The lake was calm the day he drowned," Alex explained. "The authorities didn't find any evidence of foul play. They assumed he must've tripped over something and gone over the edge."

Claire slumped forward, her elbows resting on the table. "Is there any mention of Xavier?"

"Yes. They looked into him, primarily because he was the sole heir. He had an alibi for that timeframe. He and his wife, Veronica, had checked in at a posh, private resort on the coast, just north of Seaside. They were recently married and enjoying a romantic weekend away. She claimed the two of them were together the entire time. Front-desk staff was able to corroborate that he signed the paperwork at check-in. Later in the evening there's security camera footage of him in the lobby. He'd stopped at the desk to ask for a late checkout. A few hours after that, he ordered room service. The waiter testified that Xavier answered the door, gave him a hefty tip."

"Silver Lake isn't that far away from Seaside," she said. She mentally calculated an hour or so each way.

"It isn't," he agreed. "Yet his presence at the resort was irrefutable. By that point, George had put Xavier through college and had been mentoring him to take over. He ran George's company for a few years and then sold it, looking for a new endeavor. It looks like that's when he partnered with Jared and bought the hotel chain."

Claire pinched the bridge of her nose. "Maybe it really was an accident. Unlike Jared, it's not as if someone could've crept up on him and pushed him in. Not if he was in a boat."

"It's possible that George's death was an accident and

Xavier—" Alex paused, as if trying to choose his words carefully "—used his death as inspiration."

"Maybe." Claire wasn't necessarily convinced. "It seems like a terribly convenient coincidence that George drowned once Xavier was poised to take over the company."

"It does," Alex agreed. "However, toxicology reports were run. There was no alcohol in his system, which could've contributed to falling in. Nor was there any sign of him being drugged. You said yourself, it's not as though Xavier could've sent a hit man after him. George would've seen him coming."

"We're back to square one," Claire said dejectedly. Thunder rumbled, vibrating the windowpanes.

"Not necessarily. Mason asked if I'd like him to forward this to police headquarters. He'd send it as an encrypted message, just as he did with the first file. I told him I'd check with you and get back to him."

Claire nodded slowly. "Please, have him do it. If nothing else, perhaps they'll look into George's case again. If Xavier did have something to do with George's death, he shouldn't be allowed to get away with it."

Alex picked up his phone and sent off a quick text. "Consider it done."

That night the rain continued to fall. The blowing wind and the rumble of thunder weren't what kept Alex awake. He had too many things on his mind. His conversation with Claire the night before was at the forefront. It had felt good to open up to her, to be honest about the past and to apologize.

He knew it wouldn't take the hurt away, but he hoped it would help her to understand he'd never meant to hurt her.

Mason had called him after dinner to let him know

his contact at the department had come through for him. He confirmed that the local PD had received what they considered an "interesting" file from Claire, along with a second email from an unidentified source that detailed Xavier's past.

He could confirm that an investigation into Xavier's business dealings had been launched but, as of yet, he couldn't confirm whether or not he was a murder suspect.

Alex had never been the sort of person who was good at exhibiting patience. He was anxious to check out Claire's home. They needed something concrete against Xavier and he was certain that Jared was the key.

After hearing Mia's voice, he couldn't stop thinking about her, couldn't wait to meet her. To hold her. To give her piggyback rides and to take her to the park. He wanted so badly to be a permanent part of her life.

He reached for his phone and his wallet. Using the flashlight app, he studied the picture Claire had given him. The adorable face of his daughter was already emblazoned in his memory. He still couldn't stop looking at the photo, keenly aware of the feeling of love that swirled through him.

He knew it was in part for the child he hadn't even met, but as he stared at the photo of mother and daughter, he knew his old feelings had never died. In the picture Mia had her arms wrapped around Claire's neck. His little girl was giving her laughing mother a kiss on her cheek.

Mother and daughter. They were perfection. They represented hope and love. The solidity of family. They represented all that was good in the world. Looking back, it was almost hard to recall how he had strayed so far from what was important. He never wanted to be that person again.

He tucked the photo back in his wallet.

Sleep had been eluding him for hours and it had nothing to do with the couch being a foot too short. He didn't think it was likely he'd doze off anytime soon. In spite of the rain, he decided tonight was the night he would check out Claire's home. Claire would be safe—as safe as she could be, under the circumstances—with Roscoe left behind for protection.

As quietly as he could, he got up and got dressed. He didn't want her to worry if she awoke and discovered that he'd gone. The notepad Mason's sister had used sat in a basket on the kitchen counter. He quietly shuffled across the living room, intending to leave a note.

What he hadn't expected was to see a dim light pressing through the crack under the closed guest room door. He veered toward the bedrooms instead of the kitchen. From the hallway he detected the low murmur of Claire's voice. Was she on the phone? Would she have dared to call Beth? Someone else? He realized it had been a lot of years since they'd been together. He no longer knew who her friends were. Was there someone else she was close to?

Speaking with anyone could be dangerous. Without intending to, it would be easy to slip up and give away their location. He leaned into the door, trying to make out her words. Roscoe yipped happily from the other side and a moment later the door swung open.

"Alex?" Claire frowned. "What are you doing up? It's the middle of the night."

"I'm aware," he said lightly. "I could ask the same of you."

She shrugged. "I couldn't sleep."

He tried to peer past her, but she stood in the door frame. "Who were you talking to?"

She shrugged. "No one."

"If you called Beth, I understand," Alex said, "but I

should have Gretchen make sure it was a secure line."
It would be heartbreaking to make it this far only to be
tracked through a tapped phone line. "Though, really,
you shouldn't be contacting anyone. It could complicate
matters if they're questioned by law enforcement. I know
it's hard but—"

She held up her hand to stop his gentle rebuke. "I
didn't call Beth. I couldn't sleep so I was talking to Roscoe. He's an excellent listener."

The dog tilted his head in curiosity at the mention of
his name.

Alex arched an eyebrow. "What matter is so pressing
you needed to discuss it with the dog?"

"If you want the truth, I keep dreaming about the night
I found Jared. I keep reliving finding him, jumping in the
pool. In my nightmares I always feel like I'm drowning. I
was telling Roscoe all about it," she said wryly, "because
sometimes it helps to air out my feelings."

"That has to be awful."

A faraway look settled onto her face, a wrinkle wedged
between her brows. "When I manage to get him out of
the water, he's so cold…so unresponsive. But I try," she
said emphatically. "I try so hard to save him."

Alex's heart ached for her. He knew what it was like
to try to force life back into a body that wouldn't accept it. He knew the emotional trauma that caused. The
sense of failure.

Her gaze dropped to the floor, her expression a mosaic
of emotions. "Jared was not a good husband. He probably wasn't even a good person. But he didn't deserve
to die. His killer can't go free. It's not just about clearing my name," she said quietly. "His killer needs to be
brought to justice."

He slid a finger under her chin, raising her gaze to

his. Her breath caught as she looked into his eyes. He was so tempted to kiss her again. He thought she might let him, might even welcome it, but he wasn't willing to take the chance. Instead, now that he had her full attention he said, "He will be brought to justice. I'll find the proof we need."

Several silent heartbeats passed between them. His gaze dropped to her mouth. He lifted his hand and swept his knuckles gently against her cheek, brushed his thumb across the groove below her cheekbone. Then let it glide across her lips.

She narrowed her eyes at him. "Are you trying to distract me from what's really going on?"

His hand fell away as his brow scrunched in confusion.

She eyed him up and down, noting he was fully dressed. "Is that what you're up to right now? Are you planning on looking for evidence tonight?"

His conscience wouldn't allow him to lie. "Yes."

"I want to go with you."

"We've been over this. It doesn't make sense for you to go. You have too much to lose if you get caught." Alex shook his head. "I think it's a bad idea. I've memorized the floor plans you drew out for me. I can do this on my own."

"I appreciate all that you've done for me. More than you know. But this is something I need to do," she argued. "I know every square inch of my house. If there's something to be found, there's a much better chance that I'll be the one to find it."

"It's dangerous."

"I understand that. What *you* need to understand is that I can't allow you to take all the risks. It's not right."

"I don't mind."

"You should," Claire said sternly. "If we do this, we do it together."

Alex wanted to argue, was tempted to, but knew the words would be wasted. Claire was an honorable woman. She would put up a valiant fight to have her way because she thought it was the right thing to do.

"Fine. But we do things my way."

She nodded solemnly. "I'm okay with that. Afterward, I'm going to turn myself in."

Alex stared at her in disbelief. "Why would you do that?"

"You said yourself that by running, I only made myself look guilty." She tugged a hand through her tangled hair. "When I took off, it was on a whim. I panicked. I didn't really think of the consequences."

"I don't like it."

"Nor do I, but I'm not very fond of the alternative, either. I can't continue living on the run. I miss Mia so much. Maybe if I turn myself in, they'll go easy on me. They have information now that they didn't have before. Surely they've realized the Jeep was shot at. I can direct them to the hunting shack. The bullet hole will corroborate my story when I tell them Xavier sent his henchmen after me. I know it's a long shot, but maybe the gun I tossed is still in the woods. It's possible it has fingerprints on it."

Alex didn't possess Claire's confidence. Not yet.

"I need to trust that the police will do their job," she said.

"I do believe that the department wants justice, just as you do. The evidence against Xavier is mounting." He just wasn't sure if it was enough. What if Xavier had someone at the PD in his pocket? The man could hire the best lawyers.

"If I turn myself in," she continued, "I can at least see Mia when I'm out on bail."

"Claire," Alex said gently, "you need to think about this very carefully. What if they don't set bail?"

She blinked at him in confusion. He knew the moment she understood his fear. Her face crumpled.

"I'm a flight risk." She sighed. "I feel as though I'm trapped, no matter which way I turn. I keep praying and praying, asking for Him to get me out of this mess."

A quiet scoff escaped from Alex. "I know better than anyone that His timing rarely matches ours."

"'When the time is right, I, the Lord, will make it happen,'" Claire quoted.

"One of my favorite verses," he said. "It took me a lot of years to grasp the beauty of it, but now I see it as one of His greatest promises."

It seemed ludicrous that they were having this conversation, here, now, standing in the hallway in the dead of night. But the words being spoken were important ones and Alex knew he was not the only one who felt as though time was of the essence.

"Alex." Claire's voice wavered, alerting him to the significance of what she was about to say. "I need you to promise me something."

"Of course." The pained look she wore twisted his insides, making him feel raw with emotion.

"If I don't get out of this, promise me that you'll be there for Mia."

He could shower her with platitudes, promise her that she would get out of this. But that wasn't what she needed in this moment. Instead he did what she asked. "Of course I'll be there for Mia."

She released a sigh of relief. "Thank you. I'm sure you and Beth will be able to work something out."

He frowned. "Beth?"

Nodding, Claire said, "It only makes sense for Beth to take custody of Mia. She loves her like she's her own."

"I love her like she's *my* own," Alex shot back. "Because she is! I love that child and I haven't even met her yet. Why should Beth raise her?"

Claire frowned. "Mia loves Beth. She's comfortable with her. Other than me, Beth is the person Mia is closest to."

"That's not my fault," Alex said softly. Although, maybe it was. If he'd only stayed— He cut that thought off. There was no going back to change things. But moving forward, he was going to do his best to do everything right. "She doesn't love me because she doesn't know me."

"Alex," Claire said, her tone apologetic but stubborn, "it doesn't make sense for you to have custody of Mia. What would you do with her when you have an assignment? Take her out of the country with you? Leave her with a nanny for weeks on end?"

Of course not. That would be ludicrous, he realized. "I'd figure something out."

"Beth works from home," Claire pressed on. "Her schedule is completely flexible. She knows Mia's preschool teacher and is friends with her Sunday School teacher. It's a better fit."

To be honest, he and Beth had always gotten along just fine. In fact, he'd venture to say they liked each other. He was sure that, should the worst-case scenario happen, he and Beth could work something out between them. Most likely Beth would be willing to take Mia when Alex had to leave the state.

Yet it was the principle of the matter that irked him.

"What does this really come down to?" he demanded. "Is this about you thinking I can't care for my own daughter?"

She slumped against the door frame. "It's about wanting what's best for her."

"And you don't think that's me."

Her silence was his answer.

"You know what? I'm not going to fight with you about this," he said.

Her tension visibly eased. "I'm glad you agree."

"Oh, no," he scoffed. "I don't agree. Not at all. Now I'm more determined than ever to clear your name so we can move on with our lives. So *I* can move on with my daughter."

He pivoted and stormed off down the hallway.

"Alex, where are you going?" Claire demanded as she hurried after him.

He looked over his shoulder and said, "I've had enough of this. I want to see my little girl. I want to meet her, and raise her, and be a part of her life. The fastest way to make that happen is to clear your name." He paused just a moment before saying, "And the only way I can see making that happen is to go to your house and find the proof that we need."

# ELEVEN

As they coasted down the Hendersons' driveway, the windshield wipers beat frantically, trying to keep up with the deluge. Miserable as it was, Claire thought maybe it was the perfect time for their endeavor. If she and Alex were miserable, anyone else out on this stormy night would be miserable, as well.

Hopefully they would be too miserable to even be outside at this time of night.

Though they'd foraged through Mason's closets and scrounged up some rain gear, their feet had gotten soaked as they'd darted across his driveway. The waterproof jackets were bulky and uncomfortable. Claire knew she'd appreciate hers once she was trekking through the woods.

If anyone was keeping watch, the pounding rain provided some cover as it pelted down in a sideways sheet. The truck wouldn't be visible from the road. Not that she could imagine anyone being out right now.

"Are you ready?" Alex asked.

"Yes, I'm ready," Claire said determinedly. She reached for her door handle and slid out into the storm.

Alex jogged alongside her as they entered the ridge of trees that ran behind the houses. They stayed near the edge, skirting the other residences as they hurried. It was dark, the moon and stars hidden behind clouds, but they found their way easily enough.

Claire's heart hammered at the sight of her former home. After all that had happened, she couldn't imagine spending another night there. They silently hurried across the muddy, slippery backyard. Claire kept her eyes averted, away from the pool she'd had drained.

She led the way to the entry door on the backside of the garage. They huddled close to the house, trying to stay under the protection of the eave. Her waterproof jacket crunched as she lifted her key to the doorknob. A red light blinked on the keypad, warning the alarm was engaged. She glanced at Alex. He gave her a reassuring nod. He'd gotten the all-clear from Mason just minutes ago, but she was still a bundle of nerves. Pulling in a deep breath, she stuffed the key into the lock and turned. With a twist of the knob, the door swung open.

And the red light continued to blink. They had access and the alarm remained engaged.

"It worked!" She slapped a hand over her pounding heart.

Alex grinned. "Never doubt Mason."

They stepped into the cool but dry garage. Leaving the lights off, they each switched on the flashlights they'd taken from Mason's.

"When we get inside, remember not to shine the light toward the windows," Alex reminded her.

Claire nodded. She'd shut all the blinds shortly after Jared's death. A cluster of reporters had showed up, camped out on her lawn. Not wanting to give them anything to look at, she'd done what she could to be certain they couldn't see inside.

Alex took the lead again, this time entering the house. Claire quickly shrugged out of the bulky jacket and hung it on the coat tree in the entry. Alex followed suit as it would be much easier to move around without them.

"His office is this way." Though she kept her voice low, she felt as though her words echoed through the house. "While you're busy in there, I'm going to go upstairs. Maybe he tucked something away in the bedroom closet or his dresser."

"I don't like the idea of us separating," Alex warned.

"We can get through the rooms twice as fast."

"Fine," he relented. "I'll come upstairs when I'm done."

They reached Jared's office. Both flashlight beams were pointed toward the floor, but a soft glow still illuminated the room.

The room was large, immaculate and filled with trinkets and knickknacks that had been important to Jared. A bookcase lined the back wall. A large mahogany desk rested in front of it. There were two wingback chairs, which he used for the rare business meeting he held at home. The far wall held a large curio cabinet.

She was anxious to get upstairs. She backed away, toward the door. "The left-hand side of his desk has file drawers, but he doesn't keep many paper files anymore. I've looked through what's there but feel free to check it out for yourself. I'll be upstairs."

"Be careful."

She nodded before twisting around and hurrying down the hallway.

The house had always felt too pretentious for her liking. But now she felt like a stranger in her own home. She hurried up the staircase. She had already sorted through his dresser and closet. At the time, she'd been distraught. It was possible she'd missed something.

Perhaps the same would be true for his office. Maybe Alex would find something.

She padded across the floor of the master bedroom, going straight to the closet. It was unsettling to rummage through Jared's things now that he was gone, but she had no choice. Moving quickly, yet thoroughly, she sorted through his clothes, checking pockets and empty shoeboxes, then Jared's dresser and nightstand.

She found nothing that she hadn't discovered her first time around. Not even when she swept the flashlight under the bed and double-checked under the mattress. With the master bedroom done, she moved to the spare bedrooms, doing identical searches.

As she moved to the last room on the upper level, Mia's bedroom, she heard Alex's light tread climbing the staircase. She stood in the hallway, outside her daughter's room. When he appeared, he didn't look pleased.

"I take it you didn't find anything," Claire said.

"Nothing that I would consider an insurance policy."

Claire slumped against the door frame. "That's it, then. I don't know where else to look."

"Do you think the information he compiled about the black market is the insurance he was talking about?" Alex asked. "I was hoping for something more. But maybe that's all there is."

Alex realized Claire wasn't listening to him. Something had caught her attention. Her head was cocked to the side as she stared into what he had to assume was his daughter's room.

"Alex, remember when you asked me if Jared brought any of the antiques home?"

"Yes." He edged in beside her. His gaze scanned the room, trying to determine what held her interest. The room was pink, frilly, ultra-girlie. He was sure Mia loved it. An enormous dollhouse stood in one corner, a rocking chair in the other. Her four-poster bed was covered in a lacy canopy. A row of dolls lined her pillows.

"You asked if any of the antiquities stood out."

"Did something come to mind?" he prompted. "Is it the dollhouse?" It looked Victorian to him, but as the beam of the flashlight coasted over it he thought it was probably a replica.

"The dollhouse is from Beth. This picture—" she crossed into the room to stand before it "—is from Jared."

"That strikes you as odd?" Alex moved to stand beside her.

"Jared bought gifts for Mia to give to her when he would have an audience. I can't think of a single time that he bought her something for no reason. Funny thing is, I walked in one afternoon and it was hanging on the wall. Usually he made a production of things. But not with this. He just hung it up without saying a word."

Alex's eyebrows drew together. The painting was on the creepy side. The sky was gray and ominous. Drab-looking cypress trees shot up from a dingy swamp. Tangles of moss drooped from every branch. A weathered, empty, wooden boat floated beneath them on murky green water. Alex got the impression that the passenger had fallen in.

Maybe had been eaten by alligators.

"It isn't an antique, I don't think," Claire related, "so that's why it didn't immediately come to mind when you asked."

"It doesn't exactly go with the décor of the room, now, does it?"

"No. When I tried to speak with Jared about it, which wasn't easy," Claire said, "he wouldn't hear of taking it down. I told him I was worried it would frighten Mia."

"What did he say?"

"He told me to leave it." She frowned, and Alex wondered if she replayed the conversation in her mind. From what he'd learned of Jared so far, he could only imagine how difficult it had been for her to make the request.

"Did it strike you as odd at the time?"

Claire dropped her gaze. "Not necessarily. Jared seemed to enjoy doing things that he knew would upset me. Then pointing out I could do nothing about it. The painting was such a small thing. I didn't give it too much thought."

Alex clenched his jaw and shook his head. "He liked to feel like he was in control."

"He *was* in control," Claire admitted in a shaky voice. "He never let me forget it."

Anger bubbled up in Alex's chest. Anger at himself as well as at Jared. If he hadn't walked away from Claire, she never would've met Jared. Never would've endured a miserable marriage and would definitely not be in the predicament that she was in now. He pushed away the wave of guilt that momentarily threatened to drown him.

He had to constantly remind himself he had no control over the past, couldn't change it. He needed to give it over to God and just let it go. He'd learned that lesson in the hardest way possible.

Reaching out, he squeezed Claire's hand. He wanted to do more. He wanted to pull her into his arms, to hold her close, to tell her that they belonged together. But this wasn't the time and it sure didn't feel like the place. Instead he settled for saying, "I'm so sorry for all you've been through."

She waved a hand dismissively but her sad smile told another story. "I just want this over with so I can move on."

Alex moved away from her, reached up and paused with his hands on each side of the artwork. "May I?"

"Please."

He hoisted the picture off the hook. It was heavy for a picture, likely due to the solid, gaudy gold frame. When he rested it on the ground, it stood nearly waist-high on him. Claire ran her flashlight over it, gasping when she noted an envelope taped to the backside. Her name was scrawled across the front.

She glanced at Alex with hope in her eyes as she reached for it. It was stuck to the back of the frame with heavy packaging tape. She had to pry it off slowly, taking care not to rip it, fearing she'd damage the contents.

"There's something inside," she said as she felt its bulk. Carefully she peeled the flap back. "There's a letter and two Jumpdrives." Her voice was tense with hope. "I'm pretty sure this blue one is the one from his office. The one I took the information from. I've never seen the red one."

"This has to be it," he said. "It's what we've been looking for."

He hoisted the painting back up on the wall, not wanting to leave any evidence of their visit behind.

"There's something else," Claire said. Folded up neatly with the letter was a newspaper clipping. Her eyes narrowed. "It's a piece covering the murder of a woman named Penelope Goodman. According to the date on the article, she was killed only a few weeks before Jared. She was a curator for a prestigious *antiques* gallery in Los Angeles."

"Well, if that doesn't sound suspicious," he scoffed, "I don't know what does."

Claire scanned Jared's letter before handing both pages to Alex. "His note doesn't say how Penelope is tied into this. But she has to be." She clenched the Jumpdrives in her fist as Alex read what Jared had written. The red Jumpdrive, she hoped, would hold the key to it all.

Claire,
I knew that if something happened to me, you wouldn't be able to resist taking down this hideous thing. I imagine you're relieved to be rid of me. But do me one last favor, would you? Take this information to the police. With it, they should be able to link my business partner to my untimely demise. To be honest, I didn't think he'd have the steel to do it. If you're reading this, I misjudged the snake. Make him pay.
Jared

Now that they had what they'd been searching for, he realized how much time they'd let pass. He slid the pages back in the envelope, folded it and stuffed it in his back pocket. Claire did the same with the Jumpdrives.

"We need to get out of here," he said. "We have to see what's on those storage devices. It'll be safer if we wait until we're back at Mason's."

They hurried from the room, anxious to see what sort of information Jared had provided. The man had obviously thought he'd had something worthy of taking to the police. If the newspaper clipping was any indication, hopefully he had left proof that his partner was a murderer.

Claire was visibly shaking by the time they reached the entry. She shoved her feet into her soggy shoes and grabbed her bulky jacket.

"I can't believe Jared came through for me." Astonishment colored her tone. "I know he had no idea how this would all unfold, so it wasn't his intention. But I'm grateful all the same."

Alex refrained from saying it was the least the louse could do. From everything he'd heard, Jared had been a poor excuse for a husband. The letter he'd written had even alluded to the fact.

He had more important things to worry about at the moment.

"We should've left way before now," he said. Anxiety marched a trail up and down his spine, warning him to proceed with caution. He moved to the dining room window. It overlooked the backyard. Though the window was covered, there were cracks along the side that allowed just a hint of visibility.

Rain still fell from the sky. Lightening flickered, causing the lawn and flower gardens to light up in dizzying flashes. He strained his eyes as he scoured the tree line. The hairs on the back of his neck rose when he contemplated entering the woods again.

His muscles stiffened as something caught his attention. Something had moved within the shadows. Had it been a person? Or had the wind simply rustled branches? He didn't think so. It was possible he was being overly cautious, but he was almost certain he'd spotted the silhouette of a man darting behind the thick base of a fir.

"Let's get out of here." His breath was a low hiss.

He grabbed Claire's hand. Ignoring her startled gasp of surprise, he tugged her away from the door they had entered through. They moved through the lower level of the house as quickly as they could in the darkness.

"Alex?"

"Trust me on this."

They reached the front door and he yanked it open.

Together they bolted down the front steps and raced down the long, tarred driveway toward the street.

"What are we doing?" Claire's voice quaked with fright as she glanced over her shoulder.

"I'm just about positive there were men hiding out in the trees."

He'd been ambushed a few times. It had never turned out well. Lately he might be cautious to a fault, but it would probably save his life someday.

Maybe even today.

Claire didn't ask any more questions. He knew she understood the seriousness of the situation. If Xavier had men staking out the backyard, taking an unexpected route would be their best chance at escape.

Though the Henderson home wasn't far, it felt as if it took an eternity to get there. Their wet shoes slapped against the tar in a steady rhythm. It was impossible to tell how many men there had been.

If there had been any at all.

His gun was drawn. He did continual visual sweeps of the neighborhood as they ran. He hated being so out in the open but felt there really was no other option.

When they turned down the Hendersons' driveway, he withdrew Mason's keys. With one click he unlocked the doors. He followed Claire to the passenger side.

She pulled the door open and as she leaped inside she heard a soft "pop" hiss through the air. The bullet flew over the hood, hitting a tree on the other side, throwing chunks of bark into the air.

"Get down!" Alex shouted as he slammed the door behind her. He caught a glimpse of a figure in black, darting behind a tree. Alex returned fire as he raced to the driver's side and hopped in.

He jammed the key into the ignition. In seconds they

were tearing out of the driveway. The tires squealed against the wet asphalt. He didn't slow down. If there was one gunman, he didn't doubt there would be more following.

Claire's head swiveled around as Alex drove. "There were others. I saw at least two more men running across the Hendersons' backyard."

"I'm not surprised. Whatever is on those Jumpdrives, Xavier wants."

Her tone was frantic. "Why didn't they ambush us when we went in?"

"I think—" Alex reasoned out as he sped onto a main road "—they were hoping you would find the insurance policy Jared warned Xavier about."

"How did you know they were there?"

"I had a feeling." Some would call it gut instinct. Some would call it intuition. He knew what it really was. The still, small voice of God warning him to be careful. He'd learned to rely on that voice many times over the years.

Mason had canvassed the neighborhood during the day, giving the all-clear. But Xavier's men had correctly figured a nighttime break-in was more likely.

He continuously glanced in the rearview mirror. The housing development loomed behind them as he sped toward town. He was no longer wary of being pulled over by the police. In fact, he would welcome it. Hopefully they had the evidence that would clear Claire. At the very least, they had a hand-written note from Jared, stating he suspected his business partner was going to come after him. That had to count for something.

"Where are we going?" Claire asked with a frown.

"I'm heading downtown," Alex admitted. He felt safer there than on a deserted road. He glanced at the mirror again and frowned. "Except I don't think we're being followed."

Claire corkscrewed her neck to peer out the back window. "Is that a bad thing?"

"It's surprising," Alex admitted.

"Maybe it's taking them a while to get to their vehicle."

"That could be," he agreed. "Or maybe they took down the license plate number and plan on tracking us that way."

"We can't go back to Mason's," Claire said. "Not if they track the plate."

Alex winced. "Well, about that. After I dropped Mason off at the airport I took the liberty of switching out his plates." He'd driven by a closed used-car dealership and had made a hasty decision. It was one he did not regret.

Claire frowned. "Why would you do that?"

"It was for his safety. If Xavier's men caught up to us, and they realized Mason was helping us, what do you think they'd do?"

"They'd go after him, probably kill him," Claire said without hesitation. "You didn't want them to be able to track Mason down."

"Right," he agreed. He made a few loops around the downtown area, staying clear of the police department but close enough that they could get there quickly. Finally, he was satisfied that they had definitely not been followed. He turned the vehicle in the direction of his friend's house. "Looks like the switch worked in our favor because now we can go back to Mason's, look at that evidence and hopefully have your name cleared by morning."

# TWELVE

Claire's heart pounded painfully in her chest as they walked through Mason's front door. For the first time in weeks her erratic heartbeat was due to excitement rather than fear. After several long, agonizing weeks, the end was in sight.

Alex had taken a roundabout way back to Mason's. This early in the morning, traffic was light, and a tail would've been easy to spot. He was confident they'd made it back without being followed.

"I'll get the laptop ready," Alex said as he took a seat at the table.

Roscoe made a grumbling sound.

"I'll take care of our boy," Claire said.

She filled Roscoe's makeshift food and water bowls. The dog drank thirstily when she set them on the floor. She gave him a grateful pat before moving to the kitchen table.

She glanced longingly at the coffee maker. She'd gotten very little sleep and dawn would break soon. She decided taking the time to make a pot would be a luxury they couldn't afford. She wanted to see what was on those storage devices and that took precedence over everything else. Even her lingering exhaustion.

"Is it just me," Alex asked in frustration, "or does this seem to be taking longer than usual for this computer to load?" He tapped his hands against the table restlessly.

It did feel like it was taking forever, but Claire thought it was probably the intensity of the situation rather than the actual laptop.

"Here we go," Alex murmured.

Claire wrapped her arms around her stomach. She was so anxious to be done with this. If Jared's information was as valuable as she hoped, maybe all charges against her would be dropped immediately. It was possible Mia could be back in her arms by tonight.

*Please, God. Please let this be the proof we need.*

The computer was finally ready. Alex connected the blue Jumpdrive. With a few clicks, the screen filled with files.

"That's the one I took information from, the one that used to be in his desk drawer," she confirmed. After spending a few seconds scanning the file names she said, "I've read through all of those. There's nothing new. I'm sure the police will be happy to have it. Put the other one in."

Alex did as directed.

Unlike the other Jumpdrive, this one contained a single file.

He glanced at Claire with raised eyebrows. "It's an audio file. Are you ready for this?"

She pressed her fingers to her lips and nodded.

With another click, a voice flowed from the speakers.

"Jared," Claire whispered. Though she'd expected it, hearing a dead man twisted her up inside. A moment later she recognized Xavier's voice. The two were caught mid-argument.

They both leaned forward, anxious to hear what this

pair had to say. Xavier and Jared squabbled a bit over who had the right to employ Bernard, the smuggler. Jared claimed he didn't steal Bernard from Xavier, but rather that Bernard had approached him because he no longer trusted Xavier. The reason he no longer trusted Xavier was that he believed his boss had killed Vincent Monroe, the man in charge of deliveries.

*"I understand why you did it,"* Jared's recorded voice said amiably. *"You have millions at stake here. When the delivery man is running off with the deliveries, and probably fencing them on his own, he should pay."* Jared chuckled. *"It's not as if you can turn him in to the authorities. I guess you had to ice him. Fortunately he wasn't the sort of man people miss so no one has gone looking for him."*

*"You'd have iced Vincent, too,"* Xavier sneered. *"It's not like I wanted to do it. I gave him fair warning. He didn't listen. At least I made sure it happened quickly."*

They listened a few more moments before Alex paused the audio.

"Xavier had the delivery man killed because he thought he was stealing from him," Claire said, her tone breathless with excitement. "We have motive and what sounds to me like a confession, and if the authorities start looking into this guy, Vincent Monroe, they have to be able to turn up something on him."

"There's our proof right there," he agreed. He glanced at the newspaper clipping resting on the table next to the envelope.

"There're still a few more minutes of audio left," Claire said. "Even though we have enough proof already, I want to hear what else he has to say. I want to know if he killed Penelope Goodman, as well."

They were only a few more seconds into the audio

before they received the rest of the information they'd been hoping for.

*"Vincent was a lowlife no one has missed,"* Jared said. *"But Penelope? I suspect her death will come back to haunt you. A week before she was murdered she called me, asking for help. She said she wanted out. Her boss at the gallery was becoming suspicious. She said she didn't dare forge any more documents for you. I understand that believable provenance is hard to come by, so I understood your reluctance to let her go."*

Penelope had wanted out, had threatened to go to the authorities.

Over the next few minutes Jared laid it all out, explaining Xavier's part in Penelope's murder. He'd been doing some investigating, digging into Xavier's past. Xavier had hired an old acquaintance, someone he'd known on the streets in Chicago.

Tony Brunetti was a two-bit thug, had just gotten out of prison and had been readily willing to take Penelope's life for the right sum. Xavier had purchased his plane ticket, a nonstop flight from Chicago to Los Angeles. Xavier's mistake had been putting Tony up at a hotel he and Jared owned.

Jared became suspicious when Penelope was found dead. On a hunch, he'd looked at records from the hotel they owned near Los Angeles. He'd found that Xavier had comped a room to Tony Brunetti the night of the murder. With a name to go on, Jared had been able to compile all the information he needed.

*"Tony's flight stopped in Portland on the return trip,"* Jared said. *"I think it's safe to say you met up with him. Paid him cash. Sent him on his way. You know why I think that? You had fifty grand withdrawn from an offshore account just the day before. The day after he returned*

*to Chicago, he bought a new sports car. You know how he paid for it? Cash."*

*"Don't cross me, Jared,"* Xavier warned. *"It never ends well for those who do."*

The audio ended there, and a moment of silence filled the room.

Claire shook her head, feeling sorry for Penelope Goodman, a woman she'd never heard of until an hour ago. Penelope realized she was in the wrong, had wanted out, and Xavier had her killed for it. He'd also killed Vincent Monroe and Claire knew, without a doubt, he'd killed Jared, as well.

"That's it," Alex said as he shot up from his chair. "That's the information we've been looking for!" He grabbed Claire's hand and pulled her to her feet. "We did it. We found what you've been searching for. This is going to clear you. Xavier admitted to killing Vincent. I'm sure that with Jared's legwork, they'll be able to prove he killed Penelope, as well."

Claire wanted to smile but she felt numb. After all this time, could it really be over?

"Claire?" Alex brushed his fingers against her cheek.

The numbness faded at his touch and her emotions sparked to life. Excitement, relief and gratitude overwhelmed her. When Alex reached for her, she willingly went into his arms.

"Thank you!" she cried. "I never could've done this without you. I never could've made it past my own front door without alerting the police."

"We make a good team," he agreed.

She leaned back, a smile finally managing to break free. "We do, don't we?"

This time when he leaned down to kiss her, she allowed herself to become lost in the moment. She allowed herself to wonder what it would be like to have Alex kiss her like this every day for the rest of her life.

When Alex pulled away, he rested his forehead against hers. "I think, sometime soon, we need to talk about *us*."

Reality came crashing back, hitting Claire with a big dose of common sense. "What's there to talk about?" she asked.

Alex leaned his head back, a quizzical look on his face. "'What's there to talk about?'" he asked incredulously. "We have *everything* to talk about. You. Me. Our daughter. I want a chance at being the family we never had a chance to be before."

Claire frowned. Though she wanted that, too, she didn't think she was ready to risk her heart again.

"Alex," she said gently, "I need a man who can be there for me. Who loves God first, and who will put Mia and me before anything else that comes his way. I need someone who can completely commit to his family. Someone I can count on no matter what. Can you be that person?"

Alex's brow furrowed. "I…" He faded off, seeming to struggle to find a way to finish that sentence.

"That's what I was afraid of," Claire said.

"Claire—" Alex started but she cut him off.

"Running made me look guilty. I need to turn myself in as a show of faith. I need to get these files to law enforcement as soon as possible so they can clear me," she said, unwilling to have this conversation right now. His hesitation had seemed to be answer enough. She didn't have the energy to debate him. "Can I take Mason's truck?"

Alex shook his head. "I've been with you this far, I'm not sending you off on your own now. But maybe we should wait. Give law enforcement some time to get this figured out."

"Wait?" Claire asked skeptically. "Don't you think the evidence is strong enough to clear me?"

"It's definitely strong enough to clear you," Alex said.

"Then why wait? The sooner my name is cleared, the sooner we can get back to our daughter. Don't you want that?"

"Of course I do," Alex agreed. He knew she felt guilty for going on the run. Wanting to turn herself in came as no surprise to him. "Just give me a second to forward this audio file to Mason. I'll have him forward it to his contact. That way they'll have the information before you walk through the front door."

He knew how anxious she was to clear her name, to get back to their daughter. She couldn't return to Beth's until the charges were dropped. They needed to get to the police department so they could get this situation straightened out.

After he sent the file, he pocketed the thumb drives. "Let's go."

Claire didn't need him to ask her twice.

The sun was just cresting the horizon, trying to push its way through dreary gray clouds, when they stepped out Mason's front door. The pouring rain had turned to a light drizzle.

"I'd like to meet my daughter as soon as possible," he said, his voice firm as they made their way down the front steps. "I'm sure these past few weeks have been confusing for her. You probably want to have her to yourself for a while to get back into a routine. I understand if you'd like me to wait."

"I think you've waited long enough," she assured him.

Her blood chilled when three men stepped out from behind Mason's truck, weapons poised to shoot. A moment too late, Roscoe let out a warning bark from inside the house.

She felt Alex stiffen as they skidded to a stop. He reached for his gun but there wasn't enough time.

Claire opened her mouth to scream for help, though it was doubtful any of the neighbors were up yet. She could see the houses in the neighborhood through the sparse line of trees and none had lights on. She computed all of this in the second before she was hit.

She managed a yelp as she felt a sharp pain pierce her thigh. She glanced down, surprised to see a dart sticking out of her leg. She blinked at it, watching it blur in front of her eyes.

"No!" Alex growled. He reached for the dart sticking out of his leg and yanked it out before stumbling.

Claire wanted to reach for him. Wanted to help. Instead she felt the world spin—was vaguely aware of it fading away—as she crumpled helplessly to the ground.

Alex awoke to a squeal of brakes. His body rolled and nearly hit the seat in front of him. It took a few moments to pull himself from his hazy state to one of lucidity. When the vehicle lurched forward again, he realized he was being held prisoner.

His memories flooded back in a suffocating wave.

Claire? *Where was Claire?*

He whipped his head around, quickly assessing his surroundings. He was in the back end of a moving vehicle. A minivan? His hands were bound. Claire was conspicuously absent. Where could they have taken her? His heart hammered as he tried to press coherent thoughts into his mind. The last thing he could recall was Claire crumpling to the sidewalk, and the awful realization that he could do nothing to help her.

The same feeling of helplessness hit him now. He couldn't help her, couldn't save her, if he didn't know where she was. He shoved the feeling aside, willing a sense of determination to take its place. He couldn't wallow in his feelings of inadequacy. He needed to take action, needed to get moving. He needed to free himself and then figure out where Claire had been taken.

The world was still cast in hazy gray light. He realized he couldn't have been out for too long.

The vehicle jerked to another stop.

*Good*, he thought. They must still be in town if they were hitting stop signs. They coasted forward again.

The sound of tires whizzing over asphalt, along with the sound of the engine, nearly drowned out the conversation from the front seat. When he realized his captors might give something away, he strained to hear what they had to say.

"How long do you think the tranq will last?"

"Dunno. I've never used one before. Maybe I should've stuck Vasquez with a second dose after he yanked that dart out."

"He's tied up. Even if he wakes up, he won't be going anywhere."

Unless he could do something to change that, he knew they would be right. He frantically looked around the back end of the minivan. It was empty, aside from him. He continued listening to their conversation, anxious for news of Claire, as he searched for a way out of his bindings.

He maneuvered himself so he could reach under the seat. Maybe there was something—an abandoned tool, even an ice scraper—*anything* that he could use as a weapon. With his wrists wrapped together, maneuvering his hands under the seat was difficult. He readjusted, and his forearm scraped against something sharp. He pulled back, feeling with his hands, trying to find what he'd bumped into. A piece of metal jutted down from the seat frame. It had a rough edge. But would it be jagged enough to do any real damage to the rope?

Hope and determination was a powerful combination as he readjusted again. With a sawing motion, he began rubbing his restraints against the metal. He ignored the ache that crept into his shoulders as he continued to awkwardly slide his bound wrists back and forth.

"When Vazquez and Mitchell permanently disappear, no one will question it. They're already on the run. It'll look like they left the country after all."

"This would've been so much easier if we could've just taken them out in the driveway instead of messing around with tranq guns."

"The boss had a point. Blood from two bodies makes an awful mess. Leaves too much evidence. Whoever lives there would've seen blood all over the driveway, called the cops for sure. That would've blown the cover story. Who'd believe they'd taken off to Canada after leaving that much blood behind? No one. Then law enforcement would be all over that case." He grumbled, "Got to do this nice and tidy. Leave no evidence."

His cohort scoffed. "What about the kid? Think the cops will believe they left the kid behind?"

"Claire left the kid with her sister. It'll look like that was her plan all along."

Alex continued to work, relieved when he saw the thick rope had begun to fray. His joints burned as he intensified his movements.

Their plan didn't surprise him. Kill him. Kill Claire. Dump their bodies where no one would find them. If he didn't free himself of the ropes, they might pull it off.

The men were right. There was a good chance that law enforcement would assume they'd skipped the country.

Not that either one of them would ever leave without their daughter.

"We'll get rid of Vasquez. I'm glad the boss was so insistent on personally dealing with Mitchell. I've never killed a lady before. A man's gotta draw the line somewhere."

Alex frowned as he continued to saw. Back and forth. Back and forth.

The vehicle jolted to another stop. He didn't know how much time he had left. He wanted to use the traffic stops to his advantage, but they had to be nearing the edge of the city.

Xavier had proved himself to be ruthless. Alex needed to get to Claire.

"It was smart thinking to put a tracking device on that truck."

Alex winced, irritated with himself for not checking over Mason's truck. No wonder they hadn't given chase as Alex had expected them to. They'd known they could track them with the advantage of catching them unaware.

The other man scoffed. "My neck is on the line with these two. We don't deliver, we don't get paid. I hope those little plastic things Vazquez had on him are what the boss has been looking for."

Suddenly freed, Alex's hands whipped backward. He quickly shook out his fingers, trying to regain feeling. A quick pat-down confirmed the Jumpdrives, his gun, phone and keys had been taken. His gaze fell upon the black latch on the floorboard. He shoved himself as tightly against the back seat as he could while tugging on the handle. The floorboard popped up. With his free hand, he reached underneath the lifted end. He breathed a silent sigh of relief when his fingers circled around a length of cold metal. He tugged the tire iron free.

With another shriek of the brake pads, the minivan bounced to a halt.

Alex launched himself over the back seat. He swung the tire iron, letting it connect with the driver. The passenger jumped in surprise as he reached for something— probably a gun—but this time Alex was quick enough to deter him. He slammed his booted foot into the man's head.

He spotted his belongings shoved into the cup holder. He reached for them as the driver cursed and clutched at his head. The van rolled forward as his foot slid off the brake pedal. The man swayed, as if trying to gather his wits. The passenger gave himself a vigorous shake as he reached to his side again.

Gripping his belongings, Alex tugged the side door open. He leaped from the rolling vehicle, narrowly missing a car. Horns began to honk. He raced across the intersection, glancing over his shoulder before ducking behind a brick building.

The passenger had stumbled from the van. He stood in the street, gun raised, but he hesitated, as if he couldn't quite focus.

Alex rounded the corner, raced across the street. He frantically searched for a cab, running several blocks before he finally spotted one. He waved his arms, flagging it down. As he hopped in, he shot off the address for Mason's. His captors had covered too great of a distance for him to run.

While the cabbie drove him back, he activated the app he'd installed on Claire's phone. His heart raced when he realized where her captors were taking her.

As they rolled down Mason's driveway, he tossed more

than enough cash at the driver to cover the fare. He dialed 9-1-1 as he raced to Mason's truck.

When the operator answered, he gave her the address of the shack, told her that's where the police could find an abducted woman and warned that she was likely being held hostage at gunpoint.

Despite the operator's instruction to stay on the line, he hung up. He'd given them what they needed.

"Hang on, Claire," he muttered as he tore out of Mason's driveway.

The sun had finally crested the horizon. He tried not to think about how much time had lapsed since Claire had been taken. He would get to her in time.

He had to.

His phone vibrated, alerting him to a call. He assumed it was the 9-1-1 operator but answered when he realized it was Mason.

"Yeah?" he barked into the phone, steering with one hand as he headed out of town.

"I'm calling to let you know I forwarded the files to my contact," Mason said. "He was relieved to get it. I thought you'd want to know that Xavier was arrested early this morning."

Alex gripped the phone as Mason's words spun around in his head. Finally he said, "You're sure?"

"Positive." Mason paused. "I thought you'd be happy about that. What's going on?"

Alex quickly relayed the events of the morning.

"Wait. Hold up," Mason ordered. "You said they're taking Claire to their boss. But I thought Xavier was in charge of this operation. If he's in jail, who has Claire?"

"That," Alex said, "is what I want to know."

# THIRTEEN

As the trunk creaked open, Claire squinted into the sunlight. She was still groggy, her body felt as heavy as lead. She wasn't sure how long she'd been out, nor was she sure of how long she'd been awake. Time had been interminable once she'd realized she was trapped in the trunk of a car, speeding down a bumpy road.

Staring at the shaggy-haired man who'd attacked at Mason's, she almost wished she could go back to the security of the closed trunk. *Almost.*

"Look at you, wide-awake," Shaggy drawled. "Guess that means I don't have to drag you out of there. It was hard enough getting you in, you can get yourself out."

Claire thought the throbbing aches that radiated throughout her body were probably the result of being dragged down the driveway and then dumped into the trunk. Her head throbbed. Her wrists ached from tugging at her restraints.

"Where's Alex?" Her voice sounded scratchy. She tried to sit up but her body felt like a limp noodle.

"Couldn't tell ya."

"You must know," she insisted.

"I *don't* know," he said. "And even if I did, I wouldn't bother to tell you. Wouldn't do you any good to know, anyhow. You're here. He's wherever. And there's nothing either one of you can do about it."

Claire gritted her teeth. At least he didn't say Alex was dead. Although he didn't say he *wasn't*.

"Come on then." He produced a gun and prodded her in the side with it. "Get out of there. If you make me drag you out, I promise I won't be gentle."

She glared at him as she awkwardly rolled upward on her elbows. She slid one leg out of the trunk, smacked her funny bone as she tried to prop herself on the trunk's edge and then ungracefully slid the rest of the way out. When she looked around, she was startled to realize she was back at the hunting shack.

It looked every bit as desolate as she remembered it. Weathered siding. Cracked shingles. Now it sported a broken window. Had it only been a few days since she'd been here last? Since Alex had stormed back into her life? It felt like a whole lot longer than that.

Aside from the shattered window, she noticed another change.

A white Mercedes was parked in the dirt driveway.

She didn't recognize the car as Xavier's, but it certainly looked like something he would drive.

"Why did you bring me here?" she asked.

"Just following the boss's orders." He motioned toward the shack with the gun. "Now get moving."

Claire shuffled her feet as she headed toward the building.

She noted the sky had cleared to a soft shade of blue smattered with puffy white clouds. A gentle breeze rustled the leaves on the surrounding trees. Judging by the height of the sun, it was still early morning, and far too pretty of a day to die.

No. She wasn't going to die. Not today, anyway. She

would find a way out of this. Her phone had been taken. Though her hands were tied in front of her, and she couldn't reach around to grab it, she could tell the comforting bulge in her back pocket was conspicuously absent. Her captor hadn't patted her down too well, though. Of that she was certain. Because even though her phone was gone, the vial that she always wore still rested comfortingly against her chest, hiding beneath her shirt.

"How did you find us?" she demanded.

"We put a tracking device on the truck while you were inside," he scoffed. "Did you really think we'd risk losing you considering how long it took us to find you?"

"You're not going to get away with this. The cops already have a strong case against Xavier. He'll be arrested soon, if he hasn't been already," she said with a confidence she didn't feel. "Once he folds, you're going down. If you bring me back to town, right now, maybe they'll go easy on you."

"I think I'll take my chances. Get moving," he said. "The sooner I drop you off, the sooner I can get out of here."

She grudgingly moved forward again. "You're not staying?"

The man was holding a gun. Claire should be happy to see him go. However, she knew that he was nothing more than a lackey. The real danger waited for her inside the shack.

"Why would I stay?" He scowled. "I'm paid to make the delivery. The boss made it clear that she wants to deal with you herself."

Claire stumbled to a stop. "She?"

"She." Another jab to the side. "Now move it."

Claire pivoted around as the door of the shack opened. Veronica Ambrose, Xavier's wife, stepped out into the sunshine. Her blond hair was twisted into a tidy chignon. Though she wore an elegant pantsuit, she wore sensible shoes instead of her usual spiky heels. The pistol in her hand looked dainty but Claire had no doubt it was deadly. "I was starting to wonder if you would ever arrive."

"I came straight here, ma'am," Shaggy said. He dug in his pocket and produced Claire's phone. "This is the only thing she had on her."

"Get rid of it," Veronica ordered. "I don't want it."

He pocketed it again. "Is there anything else I can do for you?"

"Not now," she answered. "But I'll keep in touch."

"Where's Alex?" Claire demanded. *"Where is he?"*

Shaggy flashed a smug smile before hustling back to the car they'd arrived in.

"I'm not sure where he is," Veronica said. "But I assure you, he's being dealt with. Just as you'll be."

"Veronica, you don't have to be a part of this," Claire implored as the engine revved and Shaggy drove off. "You don't have to become involved at all. It's not too late for you to walk away."

Veronica smiled. "Is that what you think? You really are as simpleminded as your husband. Perhaps the two of you had more in common than you realized. I put this plan into motion. It would make no sense to walk away from it now."

Claire was startled by her words. "What plan? The plan to kill Jared?"

"As I said, so simpleminded. My plan was so much more complex than that."

"I don't understand."

"Of course you don't," Veronica agreed. "You don't need to. All you need to know is that I don't appreciate people standing in my way."

"I've never stood in your way," Claire said, struggling for calm. "We barely even know each other."

Veronica looked furious as she glared back at her. "You have made quite a mess of things," she said. "I should've taken you and Jared out at the same time. A horrific, fiery car accident would've done the job nicely."

Claire's heart skipped a few beats before taking off at a gallop. "You killed Jared?"

"Oh, darling, did you really think Xavier had the capacity to pull this off? Of course not. He's all talk but gets cold feet when it comes time to put ideas into action."

"You killed, George, too, didn't you?" Claire demanded, acting on a hunch.

"I did." Her words were simple, her tone bland. "I told him that I'd like to learn to fish because I wanted to surprise Xavier with a boating trip. Xavier had been feigning an interest, at my suggestion, of course. George was more than happy to drag me along."

"You pushed him overboard?"

"Yes. He tried to get back in the boat but I made sure that didn't happen. It wasn't long before his boots filled with water and dragged him down. With the help of a lifejacket, I swam to shore. His boat was found in the morning, though it took divers a few days to recover the body."

"No one suspected you?"

"Obviously not."

"Did Xavier know?"

"Of course he did. We make a wonderful team. We always have. Xavier would do anything for me. Would you believe that when we were much younger, he nearly killed someone defending my honor? Now that's love," she said decisively. "Something you would know nothing about, given Xavier's stories about your relationship with Jared."

*Much younger? Nearly killed someone? Perhaps he'd
nearly beat him to death?*

"Just how long have you and Xavier known each
other?" Claire's mind was spinning, trying to mentally
weave together past events.

"Since we were children."

"You're from Chicago?" she asked, finally unable to
keep the tremble out of her voice.

Veronica narrowed her eyes. "Someone has been doing
their research."

Claire said nothing. She'd said too much already, judging by the anger flashing across Veronica's face.

"If I ever had any doubts about disposing of you,
which I didn't," Veronica said in an icy tone, "you have
just convinced me that I'm making the right decision."

"How am I going to look guilty if I'm as dead as
Jared?" Claire asked.

"Why so many questions?" Veronica demanded. "None
of this matters now."

"It obviously matters to me," Claire bit out. "If I'm
going to die, the least you could do is tell me why."

Indecision flashed across the other woman's face.
Claire *did* want to know why. She also wanted to buy
herself some time. She needed time to think. She needed
time to come up with a plan.

As for Alex…she couldn't fathom where they could've
taken him. But she knew Veronica had to know. If only
law enforcement would arrive in time to question her.

"It's not as if I'm going to have the opportunity to tell
anyone," Claire quietly pressed.

Veronica's lips curved into a smug smile. "We knew it
was only a matter of time before you became a suspect.
The plan was to let the police charge you, and then we
were going to make you disappear. Permanently. Unfor-

tunately, we could never get you alone. Your sister was always by your side. And then the press camped out in your yard."

"If you *had* gotten to me—" Claire shivered "—wouldn't that look suspicious?"

"Not if no one ever found your body." She shook her head. "How is this for irony? We had planned to make it look as though you took off in order to evade arrest. Imagine our surprise when that's exactly what you did."

Claire blinked at her but said nothing. She understood the implications. If she hadn't gone on the run, she'd be dead by now. Her body hidden, possibly never to be found.

"We had a paper trail leading to Canada all ready to go," Veronica continued. "At first we thought we could use your disappearance to our advantage. You'd already taken off. All we needed to do was dispose of you. However, you put quite the crimp in our plans when we couldn't find you."

Her tone implied that Claire should feel guilty for causing her so much trouble.

"No one would believe that I left the country without my daughter." She clasped her bound hands in front of her. She didn't want to give Veronica the satisfaction of seeing them shake. If this woman had her way, Claire would've been dead weeks ago. The realization hit her hard. She knew God had been watching over her, but she hadn't realized just how completely.

"Of course they would've believed it. They believed you killed your husband, didn't they? Surely, if they thought you capable of cold-blooded murder, they'd think you capable of leaving your brat behind."

"You killed Jared because he interfered in Xavier's

business dealings," Claire grated out, still struggling to buy some time. "Do you feel any remorse at all for that?"

"I don't," Veronica answered simply. "The antique business was *my* baby, not Xavier's. After George died, we held an estate sale. I have to say, I was blown away by the amount his antiquities sold for. That day an idea was born. I have worked long and hard to make my business what it is today. Jared had no right to interfere."

Claire swallowed hard as she realized Jared hadn't really known *who* he'd been up against.

"Your husband was arrogant. He knew Xavier would never follow through on threats. What Jared didn't count on was *me*. Xavier tried to warn him. Jared knew the risks. Yet he continued to dig himself in deeper. He stole my clients. He stole my supplier. He stole goods right out from under us. I had every right to steal them back. As if that wasn't bad enough, he threatened us."

She shrugged, her gun glinting in the sunlight with the motion. "He left me no choice. Killing him was easy. Xavier knew that Jared liked his quiet time down by the pool most nights. He called Jared to provide a distraction. When he had his back to me, I struck." She paused. "Hopefully it will bring you comfort to know that it all happened very quickly. He never saw me coming. Quite frankly, it's possible he didn't feel a thing."

"No," Claire said, "that doesn't bring me comfort." This woman was unhinged.

Veronica frowned. "Now, to me, it seems that I did you a favor. Xavier shared his suspicions that Jared didn't know how to treat a wife. He knew your request for a divorce ended in a little visit to the ER with a fractured wrist and a concussion. That just isn't right. A man should know how to treat a lady."

"You think you did me a favor?" Claire scoffed. "You're planning to kill me."

Veronica shrugged nonchalantly. "We can't have everything now, can we? On the bright side, look at what your brat is set to inherit with both of you out of the way. So you see, I am doing you a favor. Your daughter will be set for life. You have nothing to worry about."

"What about the other people you had killed?" Claire demanded, choosing to ignore the gibe about Mia because it was more than she could deal with. "Vincent? Penelope? Who else?"

"You're a nosy one, aren't you?"

"Do you really think you're going to get away with this? When you leave a trail of bodies," Claire said in a wobbly voice, "you're bound to get caught. I wouldn't be surprised if Xavier is arrested any day now. We've compiled evidence. The police already have it in hand."

"He's already been taken in," Veronica announced.

Claire was momentarily speechless. When she found her voice she said, "Don't you think that means they'll be coming for you next?"

Veronica frowned, as if surprised by the idea. "Of course not. You see, Xavier loves me. He thinks he concocted this plan on his own. That's the funny thing about men. They're so easily manipulated. He believes he's the mastermind of this scheme. He never realized that I was feeding him ideas along the way. Not just now, but who do you think convinced him to take Uncle George up on the offer to move halfway across the country? Xavier trusts me. He'll never let me take the fall. He'll go to prison because there's no sense in both of us paying."

Veronica glanced at her gold watch. "Story time is over. I have a business to get back to. It's time to move things along." She motioned toward Claire with her gun. "Let's go for a little walk."

Every cell in Claire's body was screaming at her to run. She knew it would be a bad choice. She was no match for a bullet in her back.

She took a tentative step forward in the direction Veronica pointed.

"Do you know why I prefer drowning?" Veronica asked in a conversational tone.

"The water helps to wash away evidence?" Claire grated out.

"There is that," Veronica agreed. "But what I really appreciate is the lack of mess. Guns, knives, even beatings tend to be so…*bloody.* Why risk DNA evidence on your clothes? Or bloody footprints, fingerprints? You understand what I'm saying, don't you?"

"You like your murders to be neat and tidy." Now Claire understood why she hadn't been shot dead in the driveway. It would've been too *messy.* She clenched her jaw, unreasonably disturbed by the realization. The only reason her life had been temporarily spared was that Veronica had a penchant for *tidiness.*

"Exactly! Now don't get me wrong, I will shoot you before we reach our destination, if I must. So be warned, it would be a waste of your time to try to fight me, or to try to escape."

*If I'm going to die either way*, Claire thought frantically, *why should I make it easy for you?*

Claire felt the gun jab into her back as she hit the edge of the overgrown lawn. She continued on, moving into the forest.

"Did you know there's a pond on the property?" Veronica wondered aloud.

Claire did know. Her grandfather had come here to hunt deer, but also water fowl.

"It's almost too perfect, isn't it?" Veronica asked. "As soon as you and your ex are out of the way, I can start cleaning up the mess you've made for me."

At the mention of Alex, her heart throbbed painfully. *Please, God, watch over him. I don't believe You brought him back to me, only to take him away again.*

"People will look for us," Claire said, trying to concentrate on not falling. It was difficult to navigate the shrubbery, to keep her balance, with her hands bound. "Beth knows I'd never leave Mia."

Veronica's voice took on an edge. "Then perhaps your sister should be dealt with, as well. Your daughter, too. If the four of you vanish, it will look as though you all left together." She clicked her tongue. "I do rather like that idea."

Claire's blood sizzled. "Don't you dare threaten my daughter," she said, her voice a low warning.

Veronica laughed. "I can do whatever I wish. I'm the one in control here."

Claire continued to move through the scraggly brush. It worked to her advantage that Veronica was behind her, even if she did have a gun pointed at her back.

Her phone had been taken and Shaggy had probably patted her down looking for a gun, but he hadn't been expecting her to be hiding anything else. Her fingers dug under the neckline of her shirt. They snagged around the thin cord. She tugged at it, pulling the vial free. With her hands so tightly bound, it was difficult to get a good grip. She was grateful for Veronica's silence as they trudged through the trees. Her concentration was split between trying not to fall and trying to position the pepper spray so that she could get off one good blast.

Veronica grunted as she tripped over a rotten log.

Claire spun and saw that the other woman hadn't gone down all the way and was quickly righting herself. She knew this was the best chance she was going to get. Her hands flew out, she pressed the nozzle and the spray shot from the bottle. Veronica shrieked as Claire's foot connected with her knee.

The gun swung upward as Veronica toppled. She reflexively squeezed the trigger, shooting blind. Searing, white-hot pain tore through Claire. She stumbled backward, lost her balance and couldn't use her bound hands to break her fall. Blackness smashed through her as she crashed to the ground.

Alex had one foot on the floorboard and one foot on the gravel driveway when the blast of a gun sent him running. He leaped from the truck, heading toward the woods. He had a vague idea of where the shot had come from. But he wasn't sure how he was going to find Claire among the thick trees. He ran, anyway.

When the GPS app had showed Claire's phone on the move again, he'd almost followed it, grateful he'd thought to install the app before giving the phone to her. Now he knew he'd made the right choice by coming to the shack.

In the distance, sirens blared. He hoped an ambulance was among them.

He knew he should slow down, be more cautious. He should approach quietly to try to apprehend whoever was in the woods. His body wouldn't listen. He was fueled by raw emotion as he continued to run. He couldn't help himself. This was Claire.

Claire. The love of his life.

The mother of his child.

He wanted to call out her name but kept his jaw clenched. He scanned the area as he ran. There was nothing but trees for as far as he could see. The sound of someone in distress—a woman, by the sound of the cries—reached his ears.

If the cries were coming from Claire, that meant at least she was alive.

The agonized sound of a woman moaning became louder, leading him through the woods. He burst through a thick tangle of brush and his heart nearly stopped when he spotted her on the ground. Another woman was on her knees several yards away, scratching at her face and making guttural noises.

"Claire!" He cried out her name, but she didn't respond.

She was flat on her back, far too still, as blood seeped from a wound in her left shoulder. He tore off his T-shirt and pressed it against the wound to slow the blood loss. Judging by the location, no organs could've been hit. He didn't understand why she'd lost consciousness.

The woman, whom he now recognized as Veronica Ambrose from the pictures in the file Mason had sent, had scrambled to her feet. She tried to take a step, stumbled and toppled. Her face was crimson, covered in a shiny substance. Tears streamed down her cheeks and her eyes were nearly swollen shut. Her neck swiveled around as she blinked hard, probably trying to find an escape route.

With her vision limited, Alex didn't think she was going to go anywhere.

The sirens' wailing hit a crescendo as they reached the shack.

Once the T-shirt began to staunch the flow, he carefully began to inspect Claire for other injuries. His fingers came away covered in blood when he moved her head to the side. It took him only a moment to realize that she'd struck her head on a log.

The sudden quiet startled him. The sirens had been silenced.

He cupped his hands over his mouth and called for help. Claire needed immediate medical attention but he hated the idea of leaving her. He called once more and received a call in response.

*Dear Lord, I know I've been asking a lot from You the past few days. You've come through for me every time,* he prayed. *Please, I'm begging You, watch over Claire. Please let the bleeding stop. Please let her make a full recovery.*

He checked the wound on Claire's head. The blood continued to seep out of it. He reminded himself that head wounds bled badly. She moaned and her eyelids fluttered.

"Claire, sweetheart? Can you open your eyes for me?" he coaxed.

She blinked into the sunlight, her face creased in pain. "Alex?"

Relief swept through him like a tidal wave. Claire's voice, scratchy or not, was the most beautiful sound he'd ever heard.

"It's me. I'm here. You're going to be okay. You're going to be just fine," he said soothingly.

"Veronica," she ground out with a grimace. She tried to sit up and Alex quickly scooped his arms around her to support her.

"Veronica's not going anywhere," he assured her. "As for you, just hang tight. Help is on the way."

He took her hand, her fingers felt small and fragile in his.

"I was so afraid I was never going to see you again," she said.

"That's not something you have to be afraid of," Alex

said firmly. "Not ever. When you asked me at Mason's if I could be the man you needed me to be, I knew the answer was yes. I just wasn't sure how to convince you. I knew in that moment that I wanted to be with you and Mia for the rest of my life. I'm willing to do whatever it takes."

"Alex," Claire said, "I want to believe you. I do. But—"

"No. No excuses," Alex said firmly as the first rescue member came into view. "You're not going to talk your way out of this." He paused. "I love you, Claire. I think I've always loved you. I'm pretty sure you still love me, too."

"I do," she said. "I've been trying to fight it. I haven't been doing a very good job."

Alex grinned as the rescue team burst through the woods.

"What have we got here?" a paramedic asked as he rushed up to them.

"Gunshot wound." He reluctantly let Claire slide from his arms. The conversation might be interrupted, but it certainly wasn't over.

# FOURTEEN

Alex's heart rattled in his chest as he coasted into Beth's driveway. It was almost hard to grasp how quickly things had changed in twenty-four hours.

Claire had been sent to the hospital, where her gun-shot wound—just a graze, fortunately—had been stitched up. The doctor had determined she had a mild concussion. Knowing full well who Claire was, the doctor had suggested she take some time to recuperate before being grilled by the police. But Claire had been anxious to tell her side of the story. She'd been escorted to the station, where Alex had stayed by her side.

By the end of the day, Claire's name had been cleared. Law enforcement hadn't been too happy with Claire, or him, for being on the run. They'd expounded upon the number of hours they'd spent searching after they'd been spotted at the campground. It had taken some firm talking from Claire's lawyer to get them to move on. She pointed out that they had been about to charge an innocent woman and that they should be grateful that Claire and Alex had brought not just one but two killers to justice.

Both Veronica and Xavier had been charged with mur-der. The police felt assured they had enough evidence to convict Xavier of arranging Penelope Goodman's murder and Veronica of committing Jared's murder. They had contacted the Chicago PD in the hope of tracking down Tony Moretti. They were also looking into the disappearance of Vincent Monroe. Alex felt confident that another murder charge would be added soon.

Possibly two more once they looked into Uncle George's suspicious death once more.

They had spent hours rehashing the events of the last few weeks. By the time they'd finished at the station, they'd both been exhausted.

As much as Alex wanted to meet Mia, he had agreed to wait until morning. Claire had wanted time to speak to Mia alone, to try to explain things as best as she could to a three-year-old.

Now it was morning.

And he was about to meet his daughter.

He had anticipated jogging right up to Beth's front door. Instead he sat in his newly fixed truck, sucking in a few calming breaths.

Due to his career choice, and his years in the military, he'd faced off with some of the worst of the worst that humanity had to offer. He'd done so with a trained sense of calm.

But not now.

He was terrified of meeting his little girl.

What if she didn't like him? He had absolutely zero experience with children, let alone with being a father to one.

He realized how ridiculous he was being when Beth's front door opened. Claire stepped onto the porch and motioned him inside with her uninjured arm.

It wasn't as if he could sit there all day. He reached over to the passenger seat and grabbed the glittery pink gift bag he'd brought along.

"You can do this," he muttered under his breath as he got out of his truck. "It's just one tiny girl. How scary can she be?"

"Hey, there," Claire said as he approached the front door. "I was starting to wonder if you were ever going to show up."

Alex jiggled the gift bag. "I had to make a pit stop." *Actually, two stops*, he thought. He'd stopped to buy something for Mia, but he had something for Claire, as well.

"How are you doing?" she asked as she led him into the house.

Alex knew that Beth and Steven had gone out for brunch. They planned to do some shopping after that to allow Claire and Alex the time they needed.

"Honestly, I'm kind of a wreck. What if she doesn't like me?" Alex asked.

Claire paused in the hallway.

"She's three. Right now, she likes everybody," Claire assured him. "As soon as she gets to know you, she's going to love you. I promise. Now come on."

They reached the kitchen and Alex froze in the doorway. He had played this moment over in his mind a hundred times this past week. He thought he was prepared for it. But nothing, no amount of imagining or speculating, could've prepared him for this. He felt as if his heart exploded in his chest, as if all the air had been sucked from his lungs.

His little girl was as perfect as he'd imagined…and then some.

Claire heard Alex's breath catch.

Mia sat at the kitchen table with a stack of paper and

a box of crayons. She was so entranced with her artwork she didn't look up.

Claire gave Alex a moment. She watched as he studied their daughter. Her thick, dark hair was pulled into a ponytail. Her teeth were clamped onto her bottom lip as she concentrated. She wore a pair of striped leggings, a pink tutu and a purple sweater. She swung her bare feet as they dangled from the kitchen chair.

As usual, she hummed a nonsensical song as her crayon twirled across the page.

"I told her about you," Claire said. "She's too young to really grasp the significance of the situation. But she'll understand soon enough and she's going to be grateful to have you in her life."

Mia glanced up when she heard her mother speaking. She clenched a purple crayon in her fist as she slid her curious gaze over Alex.

"Mia, remember when I told you there's someone I'd like you to meet?" Claire asked as she crossed the room to put a hand on her shoulder. "This is Alex. Can you say hi?"

"Hi," she responded promptly. "Are you my daddy?"

"Uh…" Alex glanced at Claire, clearly surprised by Mia's bluntness. "Yes."

"I should've warned you. Preschoolers aren't very subtle," Claire said.

"That's okay. I like directness." He smiled as he pulled out a chair and took a seat. "What are you drawing?"

"A picture." She slid the paper his way. "It's a picture of Roscoe. He's smelling some flowers."

"I see that," Alex said as he studied the black-and-brown blob surrounded by purple swirls. "It's very nice."

"It's for you." She nudged the picture a few more inches closer to him.

"Thank you," he said. "I'm going to put this on my fridge as soon as I get home."

"Momma said Roscoe is your dog, too." Mia eyed him warily, as if worried he might try to take the dog away.

"That's true but I think he's really happy that he lives with you."

She nodded, pleased with his answer.

"What's that?" She pointed to the gift bag that had caught her eye.

"It's a present for you." He handed it to her.

Mia turned to Claire.

"You can open it," Claire urged.

The little girl dropped her hand into the bag. Her brow furrowed when her fingers wrapped around the gift inside. She gave it a tug and something shiny popped out.

Her eyes lit up when she held the tiara in the air for her mother to see. "It's a crown!" she squealed in delight.

"I heard you're a princess," Alex said.

She grinned and nodded as she haphazardly slid the tiara onto her head.

"Momma!" Mia said as she glanced over her shoulder. "Look! Now I look like a real princess!"

"It's very pretty," Claire said. "What do you say?"

Mia returned her attention to Alex. "Thank you."

"You're welcome. I wasn't sure if you'd like it. I've never gotten a present for a little girl before."

"You can rarely go wrong with sparkly, shiny or glittery," Claire teased. "You did good."

Mia slid out of her chair and grabbed his hand.

His eyes widened in surprise an instant before a pleased smile settled onto his face. Claire had known that Mia would warm up to Alex quickly. Their daughter had a lively, outgoing personality. But to witness it, to see Alex experience it, filled her with joy.

"Come on," Mia said as she tugged at him. "I want to show you my castle."

Alex stood, his eyes locking with Claire's. She easily read the relief, the happiness, he was feeling.

"You heard the girl," she said with a laugh. "She wants to show you her castle."

"Let's take a look then," Alex agreed.

Mia led them outside. Roscoe had been snoozing in the sunshine. When he heard the commotion, his head popped up and he trotted over. Mia gave him a few firm pats on the head before dashing across the fenced-in backyard.

Claire and Alex followed.

"Up here!" Mia shouted from the wooden structure attached to the swing set. "Watch me go down the slide."

"We're watching!" Alex called back. He leaned against the deck railing and Claire mirrored the act.

Mia zoomed down, ran around the swing set, climbed the ladder and went through the whole process over and over again. Every few minutes she stopped to give Roscoe some snuggles and straighten her tiara.

"I spoke with my lawyer this morning," Claire admitted.

Alex turned to her, a deep frown marring his features. "Why? I thought you'd been cleared? Did something happen after Beth took you home last night?"

She laid a reassuring hand on his forearm. "No. It's nothing like that. I called her. I'm set to inherit Jared's estate." She winced, thinking of the millions and wondering if he'd come across it all legally. "But I don't want it. I don't want his money. I don't want any sort of tie to him."

"That's understandable," Alex said.

"I have a lot of details to work out, but when everything is said and done, I'd like to donate the lump sum to HOPE."

Alex stared at her a moment. "Are you serious?"

"Completely," Claire said. "I know it's important to you. After hearing you and Mason discuss your work, it was so obvious that the organization is making a difference. I can't think of a better cause to donate to."

Alex nodded. "The money will be put to good use. Everyone will appreciate it, more than you could imagine."

"Look what I can do," Mia shouted from across the yard.

She did some sort of tumbling act that Claire knew was supposed to be a cartwheel. She hadn't quite mastered the skill yet. Her tiara fell off her head and she quickly swiped it off the ground and plopped it back on.

"Very nice!" Alex called to her.

Mia beamed back at him.

"I think this is going well," Claire said.

"She's a little whirlwind," Alex said proudly.

Claire laughed. "Oh, you haven't seen anything yet."

"No, I suppose not," Alex said seriously, "but I'd like to."

"I'm sorry you missed so much time with her."

"I am, too," he said. "From now on, family is going to be my top priority."

"What about your work?" Claire asked with a frown. "I understand it's important to you."

Alex laughed as Mia tried to place the tiara on Roscoe's head. The confused dog kept leaping backward, trying to get out of her way. Mia realized they were watching her. She plunked the tiara back on her own head before trotting across the yard. Roscoe lunged after her and she giggled, trying to race him.

"I made an important phone call this morning, as

well," Alex admitted. "I spent quite some time talking with Helena."

"Helena? The founder of HOPE?" Claire asked.

He nodded. "I needed to talk to her about my next assignment."

"I see." Claire pressed a smile onto her face, preparing for the moment when Alex told her he was taking off again. Possibly to parts unknown, for an undisclosed amount of time. Sure, he wanted to meet his daughter. But of course he needed to get on with his life, to get back to his job and his colleagues.

"She was pleased with the help I was able to give the new recruits," he began. "When I was at Mason's, I was able to do some mentoring for a few of our newest team members. It got me thinking, what if I could do that full-time, or close to it?"

Her brow furrowed as she took a moment to mull that over. He couldn't possibly be saying what she thought he was saying. It was almost too much to hope for.

"Instead of working in the field?" she asked.

"I might have to take an assignment here or there, hopefully nothing too far away," he said. "But I'm pretty sure I can find a balance."

"Why would you do that?" Claire's heart took off, rattling out a chaotic beat as she began to think of the possibilities. Alex had declared his love yesterday, but they hadn't had a chance to talk about it since. The rest of the day had been nothing short of chaos.

"You're the reason why, Claire. You and Mia." He turned from the railing, pulled something from his pocket and, before Claire could question him, he'd dropped to one knee. She blinked at him in surprise.

Looking up at her, he said, "I love you and I already love our little girl. I want the chance to prove it to you.

I won't let you down this time. I promise I won't," he said sincerely. He flipped open the top of the burgundy-velvet box he held. A princess-cut diamond sparkled up at Claire.

She gasped, her hand flying to her mouth.

"Hey!" Mia called as she raced across the yard. "Why are you on the ground like that?"

Alex hesitated a moment as Mia bounded up the steps, skidding to a stop next to her parents.

"I'm on bended knee," Alex said as he slid his free hand around her waist, "because I'm about to ask your mom to marry me."

Mia giggled with delight.

Alex returned his gaze to Claire. "I feel like I've loved you my whole life. I know I've made mistakes, but if you'll let me, I'll prove to you that I can do better. I can be the man that you need. Claire…" He pulled in a breath and said, "Will you marry me?"

"Momma say yes!" Mia commanded excitedly.

"Yes," Claire echoed, her laughter mixing with her tears. "I will marry you."

Alex scooped Mia into the crook of his arm as he rose to his feet. He looped his other arm around Claire. Her arms slid around them both.

Her heart felt ready to burst with happiness. It swelled, so full of love for the two people wrapped in her arms. She had wanted to believe Alex when he'd said he had changed, that things would be different. It wasn't until that moment that she really, truly, believed him.

"I'm so thankful that God led me back to you," Alex said. "I'm thankful to Him for teaching me to trust in His plan, to bend to His will. We were always meant to be a family."

He leaned over to press a kiss onto Claire's forehead.

"'Seek God in all that you do, and He will direct your path.'" Claire sighed happily. "We have so much to be thankful for."

"We do," Alex agreed. "We have a lot of work to do. We need to get planning a wedding. We'll need to look at houses, so we'll have somewhere to live after the big day. I'm thinking at least a four-bedroom. Mia needs a sibling or three."

*"Three?"* Claire laughed, pretending to be shocked but really, she couldn't think of anything she'd love more. Marrying Alex, creating a family, teaching their children to follow the ways of the Lord, had always been what she'd wanted most out of life.

She had trusted in Him and He had given her the desires of her heart.

\* \* \* \* \*

*If you enjoyed* Reunion on the Run, *look for these other books available this month from Love Inspired Suspense:*

Justice Mission *by Lynette Eason*
Rescuing His Secret Child *by Maggie K. Black*
Identity Classified *by Liz Shoaf*
Lethal Ransom *by Laurie Alice Eakes*
Undercover Jeopardy *by Kathleen Tailer*

Dear Reader,

I've always adored second-chance romance stories. I love the rich histories the characters often share. In *Reunion on the Run*, Claire and Alex have a painful past. But they also share a daughter, and the desire to get back to her drives them. Claire learned a long time ago that forgiveness can set your soul free. Alex has spent a lot of years running from his past. He's finally come to understand that true peace can only come from God. He's handed over his regrets, his fears.

Have you ever failed at something that left you feeling as if you let others down? Have you ever been entangled in regret? Alex finally realized that God's grace is greater than all our sins and our faults. It is my hope that every one of you find the same peace in the knowledge that your sins and mistakes are forgiven and forgotten.

I hope you'll join my characters and me on future adventures. You can find me on my Amity Steffen, Author Facebook page. Check in for future releases, or just stop by to hang out and say hello! I'd love to hear from you!

Blessings,
*Amity*

# COMING NEXT MONTH FROM
## Love Inspired® Suspense

### Available May 7, 2019

## ACT OF VALOR
*True Blue K-9 Unit* • by Dana Mentink

When airline employee Violet Griffin notices one passenger acting suspicious and spots drugs in another's bag, she's thrust into the crosshairs of a drug smuggling operation. But can NYPD officer Zach Jameson and his K-9 partner keep her safe?

## LONE STAR STANDOFF
*Lone Star Justice* • by Margaret Daley

Presiding over the trial of a powerful drug cartel member, Judge Aubrey Madison finds her life threatened. Now under Texas Ranger Sean McNair's protection, can the widowed single mother survive long enough to see her attackers face justice?

## RUNNING TARGET
*Coldwater Bay Intrigue* • by Elizabeth Goddard

A routine patrol turns deadly when marine deputy Bree Carrington's boat is sunk by men carrying illegal weapons. But when she runs for her life, DEA agent Quinn Strand—her ex-boyfriend—comes to her rescue. Together, can they stay alive long enough to bring down a drug ring?

## SHELTERED BY THE SOLDIER
by Lisa Harris

One year after her husband's death, Gabriella Kensington finds evidence that he may have been murdered—and now someone is coming after *her*. But with help from her late husband's best friend, soldier Liam O'Callaghan, the single mother might just avoid becoming the next victim.

## KILLER EXPOSURE
by Jessica R. Patch

When storm chaser Locke Gallagher arrives in his former girlfriend's hometown to photograph tornadoes, he doesn't expect to save Greer Montgomery from an attack—or discover he's a father. But now he has one purpose: keep Greer and their daughter out of a killer's grasp.

## ALASKAN AMBUSH
by Sarah Varland

Pursued through the wilderness after an ambush that left his partner dead, Alaska State Trooper Micah Reed stumbles on his assailants' other target—backcountry tracker Kate Dawson. And with her skills, she's just the person to help him outrun the criminals...and solve his case.

———————————

# Get 4 FREE REWARDS!

## We'll send you 2 FREE Books plus 2 FREE Mystery Gifts.

**Love Inspired® Suspense**
books feature Christian characters facing challenges to their faith... and lives.

**FREE** Value Over **$20**

---

**YES!** Please send me 2 FREE Love Inspired® Suspense novels and my 2 FREE mystery gifts (gifts are worth about $10 retail). After receiving them, if I don't wish to receive any more books, I can return the shipping statement marked "cancel." If I don't cancel, I will receive 4 brand-new novels every month and be billed just $5.24 each for the regular-print edition or $5.74 each for the larger-print edition in the U.S., or $5.74 each for the regular-print edition or $6.24 each for the larger-print edition in Canada. That's a savings of at least 13% off the cover price. It's quite a bargain! Shipping and handling is just 50¢ per book in the U.S. and 75¢ per book in Canada.* I understand that accepting the 2 free books and gifts places me under no obligation to buy anything. I can always return a shipment and cancel at any time. The free books and gifts are mine to keep no matter what I decide.

Choose one: ☐ **Love Inspired® Suspense**
**Regular-Print**
(153/353 IDN GMY5)

☐ **Love Inspired® Suspense**
**Larger-Print**
(107/307 IDN GMY5)

Name (please print)

Address                                                                                    Apt. #

City                                        State/Province                           Zip/Postal Code

### Mail to the Reader Service:
**IN U.S.A.:** P.O. Box 1341, Buffalo, NY 14240-8531
**IN CANADA:** P.O. Box 603, Fort Erie, Ontario L2A 5X3

Want to try 2 free books from another series! Call 1-800-873-8635 or visit www.ReaderService.com.

---

*Terms and prices subject to change without notice. Prices do not include sales taxes, which will be charged (if applicable) based on your state or country of residence. Canadian residents will be charged applicable taxes. Offer not valid in Quebec. This offer is limited to one order per household. Books received may not be as shown. Not valid for current subscribers to Love Inspired Suspense books. All orders subject to approval. Credit or debit balances in a customer's account(s) may be offset by any other outstanding balance owed by or to the customer. Please allow 4 to 6 weeks for delivery. Offer available while quantities last.

**Your Privacy**—The Reader Service is committed to protecting your privacy. Our Privacy Policy is available online at www.ReaderService.com or upon request from the Reader Service. We make a portion of our mailing list available to reputable third parties that offer products we believe may interest you. If you prefer that we not exchange your name with third parties, or if you wish to clarify or modify your communication preferences, please visit us at www.ReaderService.com/consumerschoice or write to us at Reader Service Preference Service, P.O. Box 9062, Buffalo, NY 14240-9062. Include your complete name and address.

LIS19R

## SPECIAL EXCERPT FROM

*A K-9 cop must keep his childhood friend alive when she finds herself in the crosshairs of a drug-smuggling operation.*

*Read on for a sneak preview of*
Act of Valor *by Dana Mentink,*
*the next exciting installment in the*
True Blue K-9 Unit *miniseries, available in May 2019*
*from Love Inspired Suspense.*

Officer Zach Jameson surveyed the throng of people congregated around the ticket counter at LaGuardia Airport. Most ignored Zach and K-9 partner, Eddie, and that suited him just fine. Two months earlier he would have greeted people with a smile, or at least a polite nod while he and Eddie did their work of scanning for potential drug smugglers. These days he struggled to keep his mind on his duty while the ever-present darkness nibbled at the edges of his soul.

Eddie plopped himself on Zach's boot. He stroked the dog's ears, trying to clear away the fog that had descended the moment he heard of his brother's death.

Zach hadn't had so much as a whiff of suspicion that his brother was in danger. His brain knew he should talk to somebody, somebody like Violet Griffin, his friend from childhood who'd reached out so many times, but his heart would not let him pass through the dark curtain.

LISEXP0419

"Just get to work," he muttered to himself as his phone rang. He checked the number.

Violet.

He considered ignoring it, but Violet didn't ever call unless she needed help, and she rarely needed anyone. Strong enough to run a ticket counter at LaGuardia and have enough energy left over to help out at Griffin's, her family's diner. She could handle belligerent customers in both arenas and bake the best apple pie he'd ever had the privilege to chow down.

It almost made him smile as he accepted the call.

"Someone's after me, Zach."

Panic rippled through their connection. Panic, from a woman who was tough as they came. "Who? Where are you?"

Her breath was shallow as if she was running.

"I'm trying to get to the break room. I can lock myself in, but I don't... I can't..." There was a clatter.

"Violet?" he shouted.

But there was no answer.

*Don't miss*
Act of Valor *by Dana Mentink,*
*available May 2019 wherever*
*Love Inspired*® Suspense books and ebooks are sold.

www.LoveInspired.com

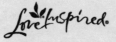

*Love Inspired*®

## Inspirational Romance to Warm Your Heart and Soul

Join our social communities to connect with other readers who share your love!

Sign up for the Love Inspired newsletter at **www.LoveInspired.com** to be the first to find out about upcoming titles, special promotions and exclusive content.

**CONNECT WITH US AT:**

Facebook.com/groups/HarlequinConnection

 Facebook.com/LoveInspiredBooks

 Twitter.com/LoveInspiredBks

LISOCIAL2018